Published by
a little book company
11 Hillsbrook Crescent
Perrystown
Dublin 12
Ireland
Tel/Fax: +353 1 455 5453
e-mail: albc@eircom.net
www: alittlebookcompany.com

This is a work of fiction based on fact. Names, characters,
incidents and dialogues are products of the author's
imagination.

ISBN 978-1-906077-06-8

Cover Design: www.johniwhite.com
Typesetting and Book Design: Glen Powell
Produced in Ireland by Betaprint Services

RIDING ★ OUT ★ THE HURRICANE

Blessings,
Maeve

Maeve Mc Mahon

a little book company

*This book is dedicated
to Eileen, Angela, Brian and Ann
with love and gratitude*

*and to thousands of New Orleans children
who were displaced from their homes
and their schools by Hurricane Katrina*

*and with thanks to Marita Conlon-McKenna,
author of the award winning book,
'Under the Hawthorn Tree,'
who loved Jade's story from the beginning
and so generously shared
her time and talent with me.*

1

Just in Case

A hurricane.

On the TV.

Orange, yellow and white bands swirling round a dark spot showed a hurricane moving from Florida into the Gulf of Mexico.

Jade Williams snapped her eyes shut to make it disappear.

What if . . .? NO!

She screeched that thought to a halt like Grandma hitting brakes at a red light. She had plans for Sunday. She would be swimming in Natasha's pool. YEAH! She could hardly wait.

Gulping down the last spoonful of oatmeal, Jade jumped up from the breakfast table and stuck the dish and spoon in the sink.

"Gonna be a big one," Grandma said, snatching her car keys from the table. "Hurry up, Jade. We're late."

Jade ran to get her schoolbag.

In the car there was no talk. Jade was thinking about her best friend, Natasha. Lucky thing! A real family. Big home. Swimming pool.

Can't wait. Can't Wait. Can't wait!

* * *

Grandma pulled up kerbside at St Albert's school. Jade brushed a kiss on her cheek, threw her school bag over her shoulder and tumbled out of the car.

"Might be late, Jade." Grandma's voice rushed to catch up with Jade as she ran through the entrance and turned left for her classroom.

Jade grabbed her books out of her locker and slipped into her desk near Natasha. She glanced over at her friend. She envied Natasha's pretty heart-shaped face, long straight hair and dark satin skin. Natasha's books were already open as Mr Cooper came into the classroom.

"Hi Jade," Natasha whispered.

Jade mouthed, "Hi". She had to get out her Social Studies books. Quick! Mr Cooper, her favourite teacher, was now standing in front of the class. He was a cool teacher with shoulder-length hair, a salt and pepper goatee and trimmed moustache. Jade loved being in his class. He usually made learning fun.

But this week was different!

Since Monday Mr Cooper had used each Social Studies period to go over weather formations, especially hurricanes. Now, Friday, he began to pass out a bundle of hurricane tracker maps. Free ones from Winn-Dixie supermarkets.

"Let's plot the path o' Hurricane Katrina," he said enthusiastically.

"Bo-ring," Natasha whispered to Jade as the teacher pulled down the all-too-familiar map showing a grid over the southern United States and the Gulf of Mexico.

"Sir, if this storm becomes a Category 5 hurricane that hits New Orleans, we're goners. The levees'll burst open and the city'll drown," announced David Seemore, the smartest kid in the class.

Mr Cooper pursed his lips. His puckered eyebrows met at the top of his long nose as if guarding a very deep thought. He played with his short beard as he usually did when he was thinking.

Jade had noticed before that he always paid attention to David Seemore's opinions. She thought for once David must have gotten it wrong. Everyone knew that strong, high levees had been built all along the Mississippi River. They protected New Orleans from rising floodwater in Lake Pontchartrain and the Gulf of Mexico. She and Natasha had often run up and down these huge mounds of mud covered in grass. They had even ridden their bikes on the flat paths on top.

"You've a point, Mr Seemore. Let's hope this hurricane'll miss New Orleans," Mr Cooper said after a few seconds of thought. "The levees aren't as good as they were. The Levee Board's short o' money. What with Iraq 'n' all." Giving his beard a final tug he added, "But that's for another day!"

Turning to the map he said, "Let's plot the path o' this hurricane."

As he marked in the latest coordinates, Jade could see clearly how the hurricane had moved further into the Gulf of Mexico, south of Louisiana.

"Hurricanes are fickle," Mr Cooper said as he stood back to look at the map. "This could all change in a matter of hours."

Jade couldn't stop herself thinking, *Every year we go through this stuff.*

When the class dragged to an end, Jade was relieved. She even offered to help Mr Cooper to collect his maps.

Just as he was leaving the room he said, "Eighth graders, keep your fingers crossed we'll all be safe this weekend."

Grandma had been talkin' about the hurricane too, Jade thought with annoyance. She didn't want anything to mess up her plans for going to Natasha's house.

"Jade, you're still comin' for a swim 'n' barbecue on Sunday, huh?" Natasha asked.

"Sure," Jade said enthusiastically. "Hurricane warnin's often come to nothin'."

"Yeah. Just hype like before," Natasha agreed as she swept her hair off her face and into a ponytail. "So I'll see you round two?"

"Okay. I'll ask Grandma when I get home from school. I'm sure she'll say yes."

* * *

When Jade arrived home, she found the door locked. She knew to go to her next-door neighbour, Mary Lou Smith, to wait for her grandmother.

She rang the doorbell. After what seemed like a long time, the old woman appeared at the inner door. She fumbled to open the metal screen door. Jade could feel herself getting impatient.

"Hi, Jade. Yer 'ome early. Come on in," Mary Lou said breathlessly, as if she had to climb a steep hill to open the outer door.

Jade moved around the storm door and pushed in past Mary Lou, who pulled the door behind her saying, as she re-locked it, "Ye can't be careful enough in this neighbourhood."

Mary Lou was a very old woman with sunken chalk cheeks, tired grey eyes and slow, deliberate movements. She followed Jade into the den, "Your Grandma must be workin' late. You hungry, Jade?"

"Starvin'."

Jade threw her schoolbag beside the sofa and went into the kitchen with Mary Lou.

"What about a peanut butter and jelly sandwich? I know you like that," the old woman said.

"Thanks, Ma'am." Jade was already opening the wrapping and taking out two slices of fresh white bread.

"Don't fix anythin' for me. I'll just have a drink now. What would you prefer: Kool-Aid or iced tea?"

"Ye have Kool-Aid? Coooool," Jade laughed at her play with words.

As long as she could remember, she was living next door to Mary Lou Smith. In fact, Mary Lou and her husband, Tom, were living on the other side of the double house when Jade's grandparents moved into the street.

Grandma often told Jade about her first day on her own in Seventh Oak Street. Grandpa had left for work at the docks. She was sitting on the floor, boxes all around, feeling very sorry for herself when the doorbell rang. Mary Lou Smith was standing there with a covered plate in her hands.

"We cooked a big pot o' Jambalaya. Thought you'd like some," she said with a big, warm smile.

"Baby, you'll never know what that meant to me. You can't forget kindness like that – ever," Grandma would say over and over.

But Jade wasn't thinking about that now! She hated having to wait for Grandma in Mary Lou's. Her house was one big, old-time clutter with a peculiar smell of dusty, ancient furniture and old cat. Not that Mary Lou had a cat of her own – but she did feed strays.

Ugh! Why can't I have a key to my own house like the other kids whose parents work? Jade thought with annoyance. Once, when she had asked for a key, Grandma had said, "Definitely not," but then she had added gently, "One day I'll tell you why."

Jade followed Mary Lou into the den to watch TV. Jerry Springer was on. Grandma preferred Oprah. "The BEST talk show!" she'd say, beaming with pride as if she had helped to raise Oprah. Jade always enjoyed watching Jerry Springer when she was waiting in Mary Lou's.

They hadn't been sitting long when two burly men had to break up a fight between two other men who were in love with the same woman.

"Jade, isn't that some bad behaviour?"

Jade nodded. She was hungry. She felt hot. *Why doesn't Mary Lou have the air condition on?* She wanted to see what would happen. Which man would the woman choose? She couldn't be bothered talking.

Mary Lou asked a few questions about school, which Jade barely answered with 'hmm-hmms' and 'uhh-uhhs'. Mary Lou often made her feel impatient.

After *The Jerry Springer Show*, Jade took out her maths books and started her homework. She hadn't finished when she heard Grandma's knock. Jumping up, she shoved her books into her bag.

*   *   *

The big hazel-green eyes that usually lit up Grandma's soft, round face were limp and lustreless. Perspiration glistened on her dark skin as she said languidly, "God, it's hot. Can't wait to get off my feet. Thanks, Miss Mary Lou. Talk to ya later."

"Bye, Miss Mary Lou," Jade squeezed out through the partly opened screen door.

"Hope this hurricane ain't comin' for us," Mary Lou shouted after them as she stood in her doorway.

"Hope not," Grandma called back over her shoulder.

For the past thirty-five years Grandma had worked in Zack's Seafood Restaurant. She began to work there part time when her own children were small. She became full time after her husband got ill and died. Everyone knew that she made the best Shrimp Po'Boys in the neighbourhood. People came from all over New Orleans to eat at Zack's.

Most week mornings Grandma opened the restaurant for the owner after she dropped Jade off at school. It meant she could finish earlier in the afternoons. Now, much later reaching home than usual, she looked very hot and bothered as she plonked herself down at the kitchen table. She kicked off her sandals, saying, "My po' feet – tired 'n' sore. All day on them in the restaurant."

Jade couldn't wait to ask the question that was uppermost in her mind – even before she had offered to get a basin of cold water for Grandma's tired feet – or had fixed her a glass of iced tea.

"Grandma, can I go to Natasha's on Sunday for a swim and a barbecue?"

Grandma's mouth became a straight line and her eyes fixed on Jade's face, "No way, Baby! I'm late today cos we had to clean out refrigerators. Left 'em empty in case the power cut off in the storm. Mr Zack boarded up the restaurant."

"We had hurricane warnin's before and nothin' happened," Jade said abruptly, in no mood to think about a hurricane.

"This one's different. Huge. In the Gulf. Far too dangerous for you to be away from home."

Jade knew that face and that voice and dropped the subject. She ran cold water into a basin, letting it fill up and run over the sides, taking her hopes with it.

Grandma had turned on the television. A man was saying something about the hurricane.

Slowly putting one foot after another into the basin of cold water that Jade had put on the floor near her chair, Grandma said, "Jade, tomorrow early, I want you to help me make groceries. We needa get some stuff."

11

Everyone's Gotta Go

"Keep your eyes open, Jade," said Grandma. "It's gonna be hard to find a spot. All N'Awlins here."

"Over there, Grandma," Jade shouted, pointing to a space beside the dumpster as they drove round to the back of the Walmart Superstore.

"Suppose somethin' better than nothin'," Grandma said as she swung her old blue Chevy into the tight spot with a loud squeak of brakes. She turned off the radio.

"The mayor said we should get outta the city," Grandma paused as if to think about what she had just said, and then added, "My old car ain't gonna take us nowhere."

With her chin at a determined angle that was very familiar to Jade, she turned to face her and said, "You okay, Baby?"

Jade would like to have evacuated but she knew by Grandma's voice that she had made her mind up, so she nodded saying, "Hmm-hmm."

When she got out of the car, she had to hold her breath because of the bad smell. It was like rotten meat mixed with sour milk.

"Ugh! No wonder there was a space here, Grandma. The dumpster stinks," Jade said, screwing her face up in disgust.

"I'll go get a grocery cart." Jade rushed ahead of Grandma wanting to put space between her and the stench. There were no carts in the usual place near the entrance to the store because so many people had come to get supplies. She waited in the cool foyer for Grandma.

"Grandma, I need a shoppin' cart. There's none there," Jade said as Grandma, wiping the perspiration off her face with a red cloth, caught up with her.

"Go look in the parkin' lot, Baby. I'll go look inside," Grandma said and headed into the packed store.

Jade walked out into the burning heat again and when she spotted a grocery cart behind a van at the edge of the parking lot, she rushed over to grab it before someone else beat her to it. As she attempted to swing it around in the direction of the store, she soon found out why it had been discarded. It was lopsided and very hard to push. One of the wheels in the front kept spinning giddily.

No wonder it was left behind, she thought as she battled to keep moving forward.

By the time she reached the rows of wilted sunflowers and daisies stacked on metal shelves outside the store, perspiration was running down her face and legs. The tiny plaits, forming cornrows in her hair, felt wet on her neck. *The temperature must be over a hundred degrees.*

Grandma was waiting inside the door of the foyer, "Jade, don't let go o' that cart. Not even for a second. I couldn't find another one inside. We'll head to the canned goods first."

Jade pushed the cart that didn't want to go straight, past CDs, DVDs, toys, clothes and household goods. The aisles were jammed with grocery carts and people bustling to get stocked up for a few days.

"I ain't never seen it like this before. Stay in one place," Grandma muttered as she helped Jade to steer the wayward cart through the aisles. They stopped at a stack of cheap breakfast cereal. Jade hung onto the handle.

Everyone was piling grocery carts with canned goods, bread, crackers, water, candles, matches and batteries. Things needed for living at home for a few days without electricity. Grandma had told Jade that the first thing to go out in a hurricane is electricity. With no electricity, there would be no light, no air conditioning and no cooking. Candles were a necessity.

Grandma carried cans of pork and beans, Vienna sausages, tuna, corn, bread, batteries, candles and matches to the cart before she said, "Jade, I'm tired, Baby. I'll hold the cart. Run and get three jars of peanut butter 'n jelly and three gallons of water." Jade noticed the number three. *Things usually come back to normal in three days*, she thought.

When she reached the peanut butter and jelly shelf she found plenty of jelly but only one jar of peanut butter left.

She began to panic as she made her way to the water. Would there be any left? There were so many people pushing near the water shelves that she mightn't be able to get any.

"Come on to the water, Grandma," she shouted as she weaved her way up the aisle to where the water was usually stacked. Her heart missed a beat when she saw an empty shelf.

"Go to the end of the aisle, water's stacked on the floor," a kind older woman told her.

Catching up with Jade, Grandma said, "Help me push the cart closer to the drinks, Baby. I'll help you to lift in some o' the water."

As Jade helped her to push and pull the contrary grocery cart, she caught sight of David Seemore, who was helping his mother load water into a cart. *Why didn't I wear my denim skirt and Nike T-shirt instead of these old shorts and this top?* Jade thought, her cheeks blazing with embarrassment. *What'll he think when he sees me pushin' this stupid cart?*

"Hi, Jade. Will you be evacuatin'?" David asked as he lifted a gallon of drinking water into his shopping cart.

"No. Grandma says we'll ride this out at home. Are you evacuatin'?"

"No, we're stayin'. We're goin' to my grandmother's – not far from you. She has a two-storey house so we can move upstairs if the water comes in. Her house never flooded before, so that's good."

"Come on, Jade. Gimme a hand," Grandma sounded impatient.

"I gotta get goin'," Jade said feeling very awkward "But hey, we'll talk again."

Doesn't Grandma see me talkin' to David? she fumed silently. She doesn't see anybody when she's all uptight. Giving the cart an angry push, Jade turned away quickly so that David wouldn't see her embarrassment.

"Bye, Jade. Keep safe," David called after her.

Jade blushed again when the grocery cart gave a big rattle and stopped. *Did David really say 'Keep safe'?* Jade asked herself, suddenly feeling warm and fuzzy. She gave a quick wave to David. Then she called out, "Grandma, will I get some cheese 'n' onion potato chips?"

"Later, Jade. Just help me with this water first," Grandma said brusquely. Jade flushed with annoyance.

As she grudgingly helped Grandma put the water into the grocery cart, Grandma said, "Was that David Seemore?"

"Yeah."

"Are they evacuatin'?"

"No."

Jade didn't feel like talking about David now. They silently pushed the cart in the direction of the checkout before Jade enquired, "Will Auntie Lynn and my cousins be staying with us for the hurricane – like the time before last?"

"No, Baby, they evacuatin'. Lynn's gonna stay in her friend Jodie's."

"Lucky thing."

"Lynn wanted us to go too but I said no. I'm not stayin' with no strangers. Anyway, our house high. We should be okay."

Annoyance raced up to the top of Jade's head and began to pound and pound. *I have feelin's too*, she thought. *I wanna evacuate.* She was trapped with Grandma. Pushing a broken grocery cart to the back of a massive line snaking halfway down the candy and chips aisle, Jade blinked back tears.

Grandma put two large bags of cheese 'n' onion potato chips into the basket with four bread rolls.

The line was moving so slowly that Jade decided to text Natasha: **? r u**

When they came to the checkout, Grandma started to count out her money. *This is so embarrassin'. Lord, please let her find the money*, Jade was thinking as Grandma kept scraping the bottom of her coin purse for pennies.

"Go leave those back, Jade," she said as she handed Jade two cans of corn.

At least she didn't send back the potato chips, Jade thought as she pushed her way back to the canned vegetables shelf.

A dark heaviness began to overcome her as she rejoined Grandma outside the checkout. They both shoved the cart that always wanted to go left out into the bright sunshine. It was a long, silent push before they turned the corner and headed to the back of the building. They smelled the dumpster before they saw it.

The sun beat down mercilessly as Jade helped Grandma put the groceries into the trunk of the car. She tried not to breathe in the fumes of rotten food from the dumpster but it was nearly impossible. *Hurry outta here*, she told herself as she worked quickly.

When she had placed the last plastic bag in the trunk, Jade rattled the empty cart to the side. She discarded it beside the dumpster as Grandma slammed shut the trunk of the car.

Sliding in the passenger side was like entering a hot oven. The plastic seat burnt her bare legs. "Ouch," she called out. She felt sorry for herself. *It isn't fair. A hurricane comin'. We aren't goin' to evacuate.*

Then envy sprang up in her heart, *Natasha's lucky. I wish I was Natasha. How will I survive ridin' out a hurricane with Grandma?* She folded her arms tightly across her chest and went into a huff.

Grandma turned on the air conditioning and opened the doors to cool the car down. After a few minutes, she closed the doors and reversed the old Chevy with a loud, drawn-out squeak of brakes.

As they drove out of the parking lot Jade's phone beeped a text. She read: **at hom nt levn**

Jade stared at the text in disbelief, *Natasha's not leavin'??*

Then she thought, *Natasha'll be okay. She lives in a big house with a downstairs and upstairs – a pool table – and loads of space. Probably some of her cousins are there too – she'll have fun.*

Feeling sorry for herself again, Jade thought, *And I'm stuck in a small house with my old grandmother. No fun.*

After a while, Jade said, "Grandma, Natasha and her family aren't evacuatin'."

"They must feel safe in their house, cos the rich usually leave," Grandma said, gently tapping Jade's knee.

Jade pushed her hand away. She didn't feel like talking anymore and she didn't want Grandma to touch her. She just knew Grandma couldn't understand how she felt.

They drove home in silence.

By the time they reached their house at 7 Seventh Oak Street, Jade's dark mood had lifted a little. She helped Grandma to unpack the groceries and stack them on the counter in the kitchen. Then she filled two big glasses with iced tea.

When she tried calling Natasha, the phone went straight to voicemail.

Jade turned on the television in the den and sat down on the brown, worn, leather sofa to sip her cool drink. Grandma joined her. The image of the hurricane in the Gulf of Mexico was on the screen again. The orange, yellow and white circles swirling around a small dark point seemed to have grown bigger.

"Why do they use orange and yellow for a dangerous storm, Grandma? Orange and yellow are happy colours. They should use red, for danger – and purple."

"Yeah. Never thought o' that," Grandma responded. Then turning to Jade she said in a no-nonsense voice, "Jade, we saw hurricanes in the Gulf many times before. We'll be alright."

Grandma's strength made Jade feel safe.

* * *

That evening, Jade's Auntie Lynn and her cousins Jerome and Steven came to the house. Jade was excited to see them, "We evacuatin', Auntie Lynn?"

She rushed to hug her Auntie Lynn. She knew not to try hugging the boys because they had pushed her away before.

Auntie Lynn was a tall, thin, wiry woman. She had café-au-lait skin and dark brown eyes which seemed to bore into your soul. She was the only black woman boss in her job so she was used to making decisions for people. At least that's what Grandma said one day.

Jade admired her because she had gone back to school to do her General Education Diploma after Jerome was born. She could be good fun. Jade liked being around her.

This evening she was wearing the denim shorts that Jade liked and a yellow Jazz and Heritage Festival T-shirt. A blue scarf was wrapped around her head. She wasn't wearing make-up. Jade always thought her Auntie Lynn looked great no matter what she wore.

The boys must have been warned to be on their best behaviour because they stood just inside the door. Lynn didn't sit down either. "Come on, Mama," she pleaded with Grandma. "This hurricane's dangerous. Please throw a few things in a bag for you and Jade and come with us to Baton Rouge."

"What part of NO do you not understand, Lynn?" Grandma said stubbornly. "Didn't I tell you, N-O?"

Puckering her brow she added, "I thought I'd die the last time we all evacuated. Do you 'member we had to sit in traffic for eight hours to get to Baton Rouge – and my knee was so sore? Anyway, this house's all I've got. It never flooded before – and I like my own bed. So the answer be still NO."

Jade was standing awkwardly on one leg. She could feel her heart drop to her ankle and make its way out through the toes of her foot onto the ground.

Lynn stared at her mother disbelievingly. The veins in the side of her neck stood out. White Linen perfume, mixed with perspiration, created a not-so-pleasant smell. In a high-pitched voice she shouted, "MAMA, DIDN'T YOU HEAR THE MAYOR ON TV? HE'LL PROBABLY CALL A MANDATORY EVACUATION AT DAWN. THAT MEANS EVERYONE'S GOTTA GO . . . IT'LL BE TOO LATE!"

Still Grandma shook her head, "NO."

"MAMA, YOU'RE A STUBBORN OLD WOMAN," Auntie Lynn yelled in frustration.

Jade suddenly felt as if her body was stuffed tightly into a vacuum-sealed bag. Stiff. No air.

Lynn turned abruptly from her mother and taking Jade's arm, pleaded, "Jade, won't you come with us?"

Jade really wanted to go with her aunt and her cousins. Her eyes flashed from her aunt to her grandmother and back again. Grandma looked old and weak. *How can I leave her all alone? Why can't she make things easier by evacuatin' with Auntie Lynn?* Jade felt so pulled. Finally, she found her voice and said in a sad semi-whisper, "I'll stay with Grandma, Auntie Lynn."

She felt a big hole inside her tight skin. Emptiness. Darkness. Fear.

Lynn's eyes blazed as she brushed a kiss on Jade's cheek and said, "Boys, kiss your Grandma and Jade goodbye."

Awkwardly, they did as they were told.

Jade found herself standing beside Grandma, waving goodbye as the car pulled away from the front door and sped out of the street. Everything happened so fast.

Grandma went back up the steps and straight into the kitchen.

Jade didn't feel like talking so she went to her bedroom and threw herself on top of her pretty pink coverlet. She pulled her teddy from her pillow and rubbed his balding head against her cheek. Teddy was always a comfort to her when she was alone and feeling sad.

Jade's thoughts wrestled each other to the ground in her mind. She couldn't stop thinking about the way Auntie Lynn had pleaded with Grandma to leave and how stubborn Grandma was in saying no. *Grandma knows her old car won't make it. We shoulda gone with Auntie Lynn. I know Grandma complained about her knee but at least the both of us woulda been safe AND it woulda been fun with Jerome and Steven.* Jade felt very angry and even resentful. She would have liked to have evacuated but . . .

It took her a long time to fall asleep that night.

III
It's Not Fair

Fingers of warm sunlight coming through the blinds on her bedroom window, gently caressed the sleep out of Jade's eyes.

Oh, we shoulda gone with Auntie Lynn, she told herself as a painful memory momentarily clouded the brightness. Then she remembered that it was Sunday and eased her body gently out of bed to get ready for church. Jade loved singing with the Gospel Choir. She especially liked the homemade cookies and punch that the Ladies' Aid served after the service.

As she walked slowly to the wardrobe, she moved in closer to get a better view of herself in the full-length mirror. People said she was tall for her age. She was often taken for a fifteen year old although she had just turned twelve at the beginning of July.

Jade began to finger the tiny zig-zagging plaits that Grandma had fixed in cornrows like those worn by the women of Africa. While she liked them, she thought that they made her ears stick out so she pressed them close into her head. And then she noticed that her nails were bitten down small. *Ugh. Need to stop that*, she fussed to herself.

She smiled at her image, saying very deliberately with full lips, "Grandma's friends say I look like her."

She pushed in closer to the mirror, all the better to see herself. Her hazel and green eyes were widely set in her pretty dark face. She knew she had the same skin colouring as Grandma. *Grandma says I'm like my Auntie Lynn on the inside with my temper and stubbornness. But I think I'm like my Grandma on the outside*, she thought to herself, examining her nose and mouth. *I have her teeth and her dimples in my chin.* She clenched her teeth together, gave a big wide smile and examined her chin closely in the mirror.

Taking a few steps back from the mirror she began to do one of her cheerleader routines. It was fun to watch herself going through the steps and to check how far her legs came off the floor when she jumped. She kicked off her slippers. *I'm much better in my bare feet.*

She had to remember to smile all the time. She noticed that she was biting her bottom lip when she was doing one of the difficult movements that involved crossing her legs as she shook her invisible pom-poms. *Smile. Smile.*

Jade loved being a cheerleader in her school. The squad had voted to make her captain and she had led them to win the district championship last year. She was in the back row because of her height but because she was strong, she had been chosen as one of the two girls supporting the final lift. Jade knew that she couldn't wobble in case she dislodged the girl being lifted up. *Natasha. My best friend. I wonder if she has her cousins over to ride out the hurricane? She has all the luck*, Jade thought enviously.

She hadn't noticed Grandma coming into her bedroom until she heard, "Jade, Baby, what ye doin'?" Grandma's round brown face looked worried and a web of wrinkles had tightened around her unusual brown eyes.

Jade suddenly felt cold. The last time she had seen Grandma's face looking so stressed was when Uncle Jordan left with the National Guard for Iraq.

Now she heard Grandma's nervous voice saying, "Jade, get dressed quickly. I need some help."

Jade had forgotten she was still in her pyjamas.

"What about church, Grandma?" she asked.

"Baby, nobody's goin' to church today. There's a

hurricane comin' our way. 150 miles per hour winds. The only people travellin' in cars today be evacuatin'."

Jade felt stuck to the spot. She kept staring at Grandma's worried face.

"Come on, Baby. Pull on your clothes. We needa pick up things in the yard. We'll put 'em in the shed," Grandma stooped to pick up Jade's teddy from the floor and put him on her pillow before she left.

Jade pulled on her underwear, T-shirt, shorts and flip-flops. She was in a daze as she followed Grandma out through the kitchen door to the back porch.

"I told Miss Mary Lou we'd close her shutters so we'll do them first," Grandma said as she walked briskly over to Mary Lou's side of the double house.

Jade followed her, feeling as empty as Grandma's shadow.

Mary Lou came to her door to watch them. She began to offer help but Grandma cut her off saying, "Miss Mary Lou, you don't have to prove nothin' to us."

That's Grandma's way of sayin', "Me 'n' Jade'll take care of you," Jade thought.

Mary Lou was too old and feeble to lift heavy things or to wrestle with stiff shutters. In fact, Jade thought she looked even more stooped since they heard that the hurricane was heading for New Orleans.

While they were closing the shutters on the front of the house, putting the rocking chairs and picnic table into the shed, cars full of people and stacked high with stuff left the neighbourhood. The Browns and the Pittmans, who lived opposite, were the last families to leave. Mrs Pittman ran over to say goodbye and to ask Grandma what she was planning to do.

"What can we do, Baby? Stay right here. God's good. He'll take care of us. Keep safe 'n' come back soon."

Mrs Pittman gave Grandma and Jade hurried, anxious hugs. Then she ran down the porch steps and squeezed into her car beside her husband. The car was piled so high with cases, clothes and food that Jade could barely see the little boy and girl in the back. Her heart was aching when the car pulled off. Her neighbourhood felt eerily deserted. Never before had she felt so terribly alone.

"I ain't never seen so many families leave the street, Jade. Come on, we have to pick up the trash cans and the two big pots. We can put them in the shed," Grandma said in her take-charge voice as she walked around to the back of the house.

Jade helped to pick up all the bits and pieces that were lying about, including a spade and a watering can.

"I hope Lynn has reached Jodie's and herself and the boys are safe," Grandma said as she took her phone out of her pocket and sent a text message.

"Jade, thank God we didn't go with them. I couldn't sit in a car for all that time with my old knee."

Jade's mood and thoughts grew dark again. *Grandma's only thinkin' of herself. Like the Pittmans and the Browns and all the other families in the street, we shoulda evacuated. What are we goin' to do now? Everyone's gone.*

IV
The Calm Before the Storm

Mr Cooper had told them in class that before a hurricane hits an area, silence wraps around it like a thick thermal blanket. Even the birds hide under this mantle. Jade always thought it was strange to talk about listening to the silence before a hurricane. The calm before the storm! But now she could hear it, sense it and feel it swaddle itself around herself and her grandmother.

"Listen to the silence," Grandma said as she and Jade stood on the porch around noon. Seventh Oak Street was deserted. The sun was an enormous ball throbbing with light in a pale blue, cloudless sky. Nothing moved.

The sunshine reflected off the white paint on their double house. It had bright green shutters and a porch wrapping around it, like arms folded on an ample bosom. Grandma always said they had the best house on Seventh Oak Street when you took Miss Mary Lou's side and theirs together. "A relic of ol' decency – a fine Southern lady," she proudly called their double.

As Jade and Grandma left the bright sunshine and went into the dark den, the swirling image of the hurricane had grown bigger. A man's voice on the TV said, "This is a monster storm. It could become a Category 5 hurricane before it makes landfall during the night or early morning. If the hurricane stays on this path, New Orleans will be in grave danger from high winds and flooding. The mayor has declared mandatory evacuation. Everyone MUST leave the city."

"Oh, my God," Grandma groaned.

Jade suddenly felt real fear. "What are we goin' to do, Grandma? Auntie Lynn's gone. Everyone's gone. You heard what the mayor said. We MUST leave."

"BABY, WE CAN'T! DIDN'T I TELL YOU WE CAN'T?" Grandma exploded. "Go get Miss Mary Lou. She needs to be with us. We've enough red beans and rice for all of us. A dangerous hurricane – hurry!" Grandma ordered as she turned towards the kitchen.

Jade couldn't stop the quick suck of the back of her teeth with disgust when she heard Mary Lou's name. *Why do we have to bring her into our house? She has her own folks. Where is that nephew she's always braggin' about? Why doesn't he come get her? Bein' with Grandma by myself for a hurricane is bad enough, but with Mary Lou Smith as well . . . It's not fair!* Jade thought angrily.

These barbed thoughts kept Jade pinned to the same spot until Grandma's no-nonsense voice cut into her negative thinking and pushed her towards the door, "Do as you're told, Jade. This be no time to argue."

Tightness gripped the back of Jade's throat. Her lips began to quiver uncontrollably. Tears welled up in her eyes. *What's goin' to happen to us?*

*　　*　　*

Mary Lou was sitting outside her side of the double house in her wheelchair. She often wheeled herself out to the porch when her legs couldn't move another inch and her feet were very sore.

Now she was holding her head in her thin, bony hands. Her long grey hair, which was usually tied back, was falling over her face and hands in damp strands. Sobs rocked her frail body.

Jade felt torn between her unkind thoughts and the sight of an old woman in distress. "What's wrong,

Miss Mary Lou?" she asked, feeling as if she had stumbled into her neighbour's private world.

Mary Lou squinted up at her through reddened, tear-filled eyes, "I feel so old and helpless, Jade. Age is a cruel thing – it sits on my shoulder since Tom died. It whispers sad things into my ear all day long. It fills me with bitterness and regret—"

"Grandma sent me to get you," Jade's words interrupted Mary Lou. She knew what she was doing. She didn't want to hear an old woman share her intimate thoughts. She didn't know what to do with Mary Lou's weakness.

"Grandma says this hurricane's dangerous. You'll be safer with us," Jade said gruffly. She wasn't used to dealing with an adult who was crying.

"Oh, I wish God would take me," Mary Lou whimpered.

Jade grabbed the handles of the wheelchair and spun it in an arc towards the side of the house where she lived with Grandma. When Mary Lou talked like that, a stern demon perched himself in Jade's heart and she said curtly, "You'll only go when God says so!"

As she pushed her neighbour's wheelchair into the den, Grandma called out from the kitchen, "Come on, Miss Mary Lou. Did Jade help you to get a few things together?"

Seeing the state of her friend and noticing that she didn't have a bag with her, Grandma said, "Let me help you stick a few things into a bag, Miss Mary Lou. We're in this together."

"Bernice, I'm done! I'm terrified o' this hurricane. I was just saying to Jade that I can't shake off the sadness since Tom died," Mary Lou's lower lip quivered as she whispered, "I'm only a burden on everyone now."

Gently taking the handle of the wheelchair from Jade, Grandma said, "Don't talk like that, Miss Mary Lou. You'll be safe with me 'n' Jade."

Jade turned away from the two older women. She didn't want Grandma and Mary Lou to see her face. Grandma wouldn't understand that Mary Lou Smith got on her nerves when she began that old talk about being a nuisance. *Lookin' for sympathy, that's all*, Jade told herself angrily.

But she's a very old woman . . . A kinder voice inside whispered.

As Grandma pushed her friend's wheelchair out the door, Jade sat down in front of the television, feeling ashamed at the way she had treated her old neighbour. On the TV a meteorologist announced, "Hurricane Katrina may be 'The Big One' that everyone has dreaded. A monster hurricane is heading

34

towards New Orleans. Over a million people are clogging up all roads leaving the city."

Jade couldn't stop icy fingers of fear gripping her heart, making it difficult for her to breathe.

V

Mary Lou

"The weather's changin'," Mary Lou said as she came into the den, linking Grandma with one arm and carrying her big black bag on the other.

Jade noticed that Mary Lou's long grey hair was combed and tied back. She had changed from her loose dress into her black pants, white blouse and black cardigan.

"Great dark clouds are blockin' out the sun. I caught the weather just now at two on the TV. The good news is Hurricane Katrina is expected to make landfall east o' N'Awlins," Mary Lou said breathlessly. She shuffled into the kitchen and sat in her usual place at the kitchen table.

Jade was still resenting the fact that Mary Lou was in their house for the hurricane so she pretended not to notice her. Instead, she looked at Grandma, who had gone to the stove to heat up the red beans and rice. She heard Mary Lou ask, "Bernice, should we go to the Superdome? The mayor has opened it for the people who can't leave the city. Would we be safer there?"

Jade began to feel more positive. *Yeah, we should go to the Superdome.* She had heard her Grandma and Mary Lou talking about how there was no electricity during Hurricane Betsy. Food rotted in refrigerators and the heat was intolerable when there was no air conditioning. *The Superdome will be air conditioned and the Red Cross will feed us.* Jade's spirits lifted.

Grandma's round, soft face looked pinched with worry. She answered her old friend in a low, thin voice, "I think we'll be safer here, Miss Mary Lou. This house never flooded before. We've enough food in for a few days. Might be a rough crowd in the Superdome."

"I guess you're right. Did I bring my water pills?" Mary Lou said distractedly as she searched in her big black bag.

Jade's heart sank. Down. Down. Down. Grandma had not changed her mind. They would not be leaving.

* * *

Over the years, Grandma had reminded Jade many times that their neighbour was very old and deserved respect. She'd worked hard in factories all her life. When she retired, things should have been a little easier for her but her husband got cancer. After nine months of being in and out of the hospital, he died.

"Losin' Mr Tom was bad – what with no kids 'n' all," Grandma said when she first heard that her neighbour had died. "Po' Miss Mary Lou always wanted kids but couldn't have none."

When Jade asked if she had any family, Grandma said, "Yeah. She has one nephew, Gary. He lives far away. I think he's married."

Then, giving Jade a long intense look, she had said, "We have to be family for her, Jade."

Grandma had looked so sad and serious that Jade couldn't tell her what she was really thinking: *An old white woman can never be part of my family*.

Now, Jade was glad that she hadn't said anything to upset Grandma.

*   *   *

"Jade, Baby, get three plates and serve the red beans and rice. I'll help Miss Mary Lou find her water pills."

Grandma walked over to her friend and gently

took the big black bag from her. "Here they are," she said taking a small white pillbox out of the bag and placing it near Mary Lou's plate.

Why won't Grandma go to the Superdome? What if we have no power for days and the streets flood? What will we do for food and water? The mayor said EVERYONE MUST LEAVE, Jade fretted. She tried not to suck her lips and cut her eyes but she couldn't help feeling disgusted. *Grandma doesn't seem to care.*

Dividing out the red beans and rice, Jade gave herself a small portion of each. She struggled to eat the food because her mouth was dry and she didn't feel hungry. Even taking a long drink of water didn't really help. When she could eat no more, she picked up the plates and brought them to the sink.

Grandma came over to her. Putting her arm around her shoulders she said, "Jade, Miss Mary Lou should spend the night with us. I told her you'd give her your bed. You can sleep with me."

WHAT! Jade felt her body fill up with anger. Her heart began to race as she tightened her shoulders under Grandma's heavy arm. *Why is Grandma lettin' a stranger sleep in my bed? Okay, she knows her, but SHE'S NOT FAMILY. I haven't slept in Grandma's bed since I was about three years old and was afraid to be left alone.*

Jade felt nervousness in her middle and awkwardness

with Grandma. She muttered some words her heart didn't feel, "Okay, Grandma."

Then she pulled away from her grandmother and went into her bedroom to straighten it up. Opening her nightstand drawer, she took out the Tiffany heart tag charm bracelet that had belonged to her Mama. It was the only thing she had of the mother who died shortly after she was born. Carefully, she put it on her left wrist.

Jade felt so alone. Nobody understood her. *Grandma sure doesn't*, Jade thought sadly.

She dialled Natasha's number but her phone was powered off.

David Seemore's number rang and rang.

No one picked up.

She scrolled down for another school friend's number and dialled Dwight Turner. There was no answer.

Finally, she lay down on her bed, took her MP3 player out of her pocket, plugged in her earphones and began to listen to her music. She was in her own little sad world.

Hours passed.

* * *

When Jade went back into the kitchen later that Sunday evening, Grandma and Mary Lou were still sitting at the kitchen table. A large candle, matches and two torches were on the table. A bowl of potato chips was beside the candle. Mary Lou was shuffling the playing cards.

"Come on, Baby. We'll play your favourite card game," Grandma said patting the chair near her for her granddaughter to sit down.

Playing cards is better than doin' nothin', Jade thought as she pulled her chair in at the table and lifted up the cards that Mary Lou had dealt her. They began to play Twenty-One. Jade was able to relax a little with Grandma and Mary Lou. It was pleasant inside with the air conditioning humming in the background and the TV on the weather station.

Outside, the dark was creeping slowly around the neighbourhood. Heavy rain beat on the shutters. The wind cried mournfully in the chimney. It rattled the shutters and developed a strange, wild howl. Then it began to shriek, wail and pull on the carport aluminium cover.

Grandma got up from the table and went to the door. She tried to open it but the wind banged it closed with ferocious force. Putting her body against the door, she bolted it and pushed the sofa behind it.

She had just sat down at the table again when a loud peal of thunder roared over the house. Bolts of lightning added frenzy to the wind.

The air conditioning shuddered loudly like a freight train screaming to a halt. The lights flickered and went out. The television gave an audible blink and shut off.

"There's the electricity gone," Mary Lou said. "Light a candle, Bernice."

Grandma lit the candle. It cast some light at the table but the rest of the house looked spooky.

One previous year when they lost power in a storm, Jade's cousin Jerome and her Uncle Jordan told ghost stories. The more she screamed to stop, the more they added scary bits. That was great fun. It was different now being with two old adults.

"Cards are a great distraction. We'll play a few more games," Grandma said bravely, the candle giving a ghost-like appearance to her face, wet with perspiration.

In the flickering candlelight, Jade thought Mary Lou looked like a corpse. The skin on the old woman's cheeks was pulled tightly around her jaws, like cheesecloth, making her teeth look too large and her lips too thin for her mouth. Jade gave an involuntary shudder. Goosebumps pushed Jade's nervous skin up in a million points. She dropped her eyes to look at the cards in her hands. It was easier to do that.

Even though Jade won eight out of the ten games as she munched mechanically on her favourite potato chips, she couldn't banish the weird feeling that she was playing cards with the living dead. *Mary Lou, I mean . . . What a terrible thought . . . Stop it*, Jade told herself sternly.

Eventually, Grandma and Mary Lou grew tired playing cards. The evening dragged on, time passing slowly and hesitantly like an old man trying to pedal a bike with a rusty chain up a very steep hill. The wind's roar and driving rain were always there in the background. Jade heard metal sheeting rip off a neighbouring house. Then came a loud crash of aluminium, glass and metal.

"That must be the carport," Grandma said in a loud whisper. "Say a prayer my car's okay."

Jade knew how much Grandma liked her old Chevy so she prayed silently, *God protect Grandma's car. You know she needs it. Amen.*

The sounds of breaking glass, ripping tin, howling winds and flying tree branches made looking outside too dangerous.

Using the light of the candle, Grandma took the

portable television out of her bedroom and put it on the counter top. Because it worked on batteries, they were able to see the nine o'clock news on WWL-TV.

Louis Armstrong International Airport was closed and newsmen were braving the hurricane winds to get pictures of the damage as it unfolded. Howling winds were ripping apart sections of colourful store awnings and sending large pieces of debris flying through the air. Some barely missed the reporters. At one intersection, a huge piece of plastic roofing spun and danced like a top.

The city was being pounded by over one hundred miles per hour winds. Grandma's house on Seventh Oak Street groaned and shook under the pressure of the gales.

Hours seemed to pass as they watched the destruction on television. Jade felt as if she was being hypnotised to keep viewing a terrible hurricane wreck their city. They were all living one big gasp of horror.

Finally, it was all too much for Jade. She began to shake and feel cold inside. "Grandma we're gonna die."

"Don't say that, Jade. God'll take care of us. This'll pass. Anyway, I think you should go to bed," Grandma pulled Jade to her bosom and gave her a long, tight hug. The warmth and comfort of Grandma's body helped her to steady up. Jade remained close to Grandma until she thought, *I can't go to bed. Grandma and Mary Lou can't go to bed either. How could we go to bed? . . . The wind might pull the roof off our house?*

Wrenching herself away from Grandma at the kitchen table, Jade jumped onto the sofa in the den. She wrapped the Afghan throw that had been draped on the back, tightly around her body as if protecting herself against an enemy that was about to batter the door in. Putting her MP3 earphones into her ears and turning the volume up high, she tried to drown out the roar of the wind but she wasn't able to turn off her thoughts.

Where is Natasha now? Why hasn't she tried to call me? Did David Seemore go to his grandmother's? If he did, he must be experiencing these strong winds. Did Dwight Turner evacuate? Maybe they all evacuated this morning when the mayor said everyone MUST LEAVE New Orleans. Mandatory Evacuation. The first time ever.

Jade sadly fingered her good luck heart charm. She hadn't left.

*   *   *

Jade didn't know she had fallen asleep until she turned on the couch and bumped into Grandma sitting beside her. She put her arm around Grandma's waist that was as round as the middle-sized oak tree in the backyard, but much softer. It was such a good feeling to nestle into Grandma's soft curves and drift off into a gentle sleep again.

Waking up suddenly, unsure where she was, Jade heard Grandma say in a loud whisper, "It's the end of the month, Miss Mary Lou. My pay cheque nearly used up. We can't afford to go nowhere."

"Anyway, I think we just dodged a bullet, Bernice. N'Awlins spared once again. The hurricane's goin' in way east of the city," Mary Lou said quite loudly.

Jade peered out through her half-closed eyelashes as she really didn't want to wake up fully. Grandma was now sitting on the opposite end of the sofa talking to Mary Lou, who had remained at the kitchen table. Jade knew that Grandma was a proud black woman. Now she had just overheard the real reason why Grandma had told Auntie Lynn she wouldn't evacuate. She had no money left and she didn't want her daughter to know! A feeling of tenderness for Grandma washed over Jade. She felt like getting up to give her a hug but restrained herself. Grandma wouldn't have wanted her to know about the money.

* * *

When Grandma moved to stand up to straighten her knee, Jade wakened up fully. *Or was it the sound of things crashing and the wind shrieking wildly that wakened me?* Jade wondered. She was sorry she was awake now. It was nice to escape for a while from the terrifying sounds outside.

"Grandma, I'm scared," she said with her heart in her mouth.

"Don't be afraid. The worst's over, Baby," Grandma whispered calmly. "I know it's dark and hot in here but at least we don't have flyin' glass to worry about."

Then they heard it. A terrible, blood-curdling scream. It seemed quite close to the house. Jade lay frozen still. *What could have happened outside?* The scream rose above the shrieks of the wind.

Mary Lou shouted from the kitchen, "Bernice, what was that?"

"It sounds like a woman screamin'," Grandma answered. She was pulling on her sandals as fast as she could.

"Sounded like it came from behind us," Jade said.

"I'll try openin' the kitchen door to the back porch," Grandma said as she half-ran towards the kitchen.

Jade grabbed the candle from the table near Mary Lou but she didn't need it as the morning light was already pushing through the wooden slats in thin, yellow, parallel lines. It was the morning of Monday 29 August 2005. Jade blew out the candle and left it down again.

Grandma prised open the back door. They were shocked to see so much destruction. The backyard was full of debris including sections of the blue and red siding of the corner washateria. They couldn't see the carport but they had heard the noise of it being ripped off the side wall when the winds were howling earlier.

Rain was falling in diagonal wet lines from a heavy grey sky. The wind had died considerably. But there was a new sound that paralysed Jade. The sound of rushing water. Water, like a river overflowing its banks, was coming towards their house.

In a matter of minutes, the back garden was a mucky, debris-strewn lake and the water was still rising.

VI

I Can't Breathe

Jade clung tightly to Grandma as they watched the angry water burst into their backyard, swirl around the large oak tree standing in the middle of the garden and submerge the small azalea bush at the side of the shed. There was nothing they could do to stop it.

"The water from the canal musta come over the levees," Grandma said in a shocked voice, her mouth hanging open in disbelief. Her brow furrowed deeply.

Jade felt her body and mind go numb. She was stuck to the spot and to Grandma.

Releasing her granddaughter's tight hold, Grandma ordered in an urgent, husky whisper, "Go get Miss Mary Lou, Jade."

Jade ran with her heart in her mouth into the house

but Mary Lou was already fully dressed, standing in the kitchen, holding her big black bag and a torch.

"The water's comin'," Jade shouted as she dashed past her into her bedroom.

Grandma's voice followed her, "Baby, put three changes of underwear, shorts and T-shirts into your school bag. And your hair gel and brush. Anything else you might want to bring if we have to leave suddenly."

Jade knew one thing that she was bringing for certain: her Mama's charm bracelet. She zipped it into the front pocket of her knapsack.

Off the top of her dresser, she took the MP3 battery charger, phone, hairbrush and gel and pushed them in among her clothes. She thought about bringing the teddy she had since she was a baby but then decided to leave him on her pillow, telling him with a lump in her throat, "Look after this place, Teddy, won't you?"

Mary Lou's frail voice asking, "What can I do to help, Bernice?" made Jade rush back to Grandma. "Check that you have your water pills and batteries for the torch, Miss Mary Lou."

"Oh, God – the water's comin' into the house." Grandma was pulling the sofa back from where she had pushed it up against the door earlier. Quickly taking off the cushions, she shoved them tightly together on the floor to try to stem the flow of water coming under the door.

Then she shouted to no one in particular, "Get some kitchen towels and put them at the back door to keep the water out."

"I'll check the back door, Grandma," Jade shouted, as she dashed to get the towels near the stove to put on the floor at the kitchen door.

Just as Jade was forming a towel barricade at the back door, she heard the bang of the trapdoor to the attic being released and the rasping sound of the ladder being pulled down.

"GRANDMA, WE CAN'T GO INTO THE ATTIC," she screamed.

Her mind flashed back to the summer day she had climbed up there to get a suitcase for Grandma. The heat was unbearable. No windows. No ventilation. By the time she had got down again, only two minutes later, she was in a pool of perspiration and her clothes were sticking to her.

"Baby, if we don't go up, we'll drown in here. Can't you see the water in the house and it's still comin'?" Grandma's voice had risen with anxiety.

Jade's heart was thumping. Her mouth and lips were dry. She began to help Grandma carry the food from the kitchen counter over to the narrow wooden steps going up steeply to the attic.

"Come on, Jade," Mary Lou shrilled. She had begun to climb slowly and painfully up the ladder to the attic, one hesitant foot after another.

"Jade, go help Miss Mary Lou get situated. Here's a torch. Don't forget your own knapsack."

Jade Williams felt as if she had stepped outside her own body. A 12-year-old stranger was climbing up to the attic behind a very old white woman. It was like going through the motions in a strange and terrifying world. They were climbing up into a furnace to escape being drowned. Life had become unreal. Jade felt suspended in a weird disaster story. Caught in a terrible trap.

The cushions and the towels couldn't hold back the brown floodwater. It was advancing in slow, wet arcs towards the bottom of the ladder and the bags of food.

"Quick, Baby. Come back 'n' help me with the food." Grandma's voice compelled Jade to rush back down the ladder once she saw Mary Lou step hesitantly into the attic.

"Gimme two bags, Grandma," Jade said as she balanced precariously on the second rung of the ladder and stretched out her hands.

"Can you manage the bottles of water, Baby? Be careful, they're heavy. Hey, take one at a time."

Jade reached for a bottle and, wrapping her arm around it as Grandma held it, pulled it into her body. She turned, struggling to get her balance. Weighted on the right side by the large bottle, she leaned into the ladder while grabbing the narrow rung above her left shoulder. She stepped up with her left foot onto the next rung and dragged her right foot up slowly after it. The heavy bottle of water was pulling her down but she forced herself to continue climbing. She held her breath. She dare not look down at Grandma for fear that she'd tumble off her perch.

"Good girl, Jade. You'll be there soon," Grandma's encouraging words made the bottle a little lighter.

As she steadied on the third rung from the top, a thick wall of heat pushed into her face forcing her to stop. She tried to raise the bottle above her shoulder but that caused her to teeter so, lowering the bottle and hugging it to her chest, she steadied herself again for one more rung. The wood felt rough under her feet and she winced as a jab of pain shot through her left instep. She leaned into the ladder, using both hands to roll the bottle through the attic opening. A flush of accomplishment now burnt her cheeks but more water had to be carried up so there was no time for pride or praise. She scrambled down the ladder to do the same thing again.

When she had heaved the second bottle into the attic, Jade summoned the strength to put her elbows on the wooden flooring and draw her body up slowly into the airless, dimly lit space. She lay immobile on her tummy on the attic floor. In the light of Mary Lou's torch, she could see her old neighbour sitting on a box. She was fanning herself with an old book she had found. The big black bag was on the floor at her feet. To the left of it, Jade could barely make out the shape of the air-conditioning pipes, snaking along like aluminium pythons where the slanted roof met the rough boxwood floor.

Old cases and boxes were stacked two deep to the right of Mary Lou. A nervous shiver ran through Jade's tired body when she realised where she was. There were times, over the past year, when she had been lying awake in the darkness of her bedroom listening to strange sounds. She had thought then that mice were running and squeaking above her in the attic. Now the mice could probably hear her heart thumping loudly through her thin T-shirt as they hid behind the air-conditioning pipes.

Fear lurked just behind Jade's eyes, drawing a veil over her sight. She couldn't see anything else in the attic. She could hear Grandma climbing slowly up the ladder and when her head appeared above the opening, Jade whispered hoarsely, "I can't breathe, Grandma."

The acrid heat had sucked the moisture out of her mouth and the back of her throat felt straw-dry. There was a distinctive smell in the attic. Insulation, old dust and dried-out wood. Her eyes started to burn as if someone had lit a match and passed it quickly along her eyelashes. Dry rasping coughs began to shake her body and she gasped for air in quick, shallow breaths.

"Grandma, I can't breathe," Jade whispered as she rolled away from the opening. She was panicking at the thought of having to stay in the boiling, airless furnace. Scrambling to her knees, she bent over and tried to fill her lungs with air.

Terror made her chest bone squash her lungs into her back bone the way bagpipes are squeezed under the piper's arm. "Aaaaaaaahhh—eeeeeeeeeee," a shriek burst out from her tense insides like the shrill squeal of a bagpipe.

Grandma had just stepped into the attic with some bags of food and her large brown holdall, "We can't stay here long, Baby. No air up here. I know what we need. You can help us, Jade."

She heaved Jade up on her feet and said in an

urgent voice, "Go down and wet three towels. We can use them to keep cool."

Grandma's strength helped Jade stand up. She was relieved to get out of the attic. Taking deep breaths to calm her nerves, she moved as quickly as she could towards the opening for the ladder. She turned herself around to go down the steps backwards, her knees trembling. When she glanced down, she was shocked to find that the water had risen so much that she couldn't see the bottom rungs.

Gingerly, she lowered herself into the water. Because she was tall for her age, the warm, dirty water came up just below her knees. *Hurry! Hurry!* She told herself.

The furniture in the den was now bouncing in the murky water and the towels she had left at the back door came floating towards her. She grabbed them and waded into the bathroom to turn on the tap for clean water.

The water spluttered and then came out as a thin brown trickle before it stopped completely. She had only two towels so she tried opening the towel closet in the bathroom to get another one, but the depth of the water made it impossible. Then she caught sight of the dry towels on the towel rack. *Two clean towels. What luck!* Dropping the dirty towels in the water, she grabbed the clean ones.

"Jaaaaaaaade. Come back quickly," Grandma had climbed down the ladder to the rung above the water. Jade could hear the concern and urgency in her voice. She waded back from the bathroom. Now the stink of sewage mixed with oil was unbearable.

"The water's stinkin', Grandma."

Holding her nose with the finger and thumb of her right hand, she pinned the towels to her side with her elbow and moved quickly to get out of the putrid water. She handed the towels up to Grandma and stepped up on the ladder behind her to climb into the attic.

To Jade, the brittle, dry, attic smell was now better than the stench below.

"Thank God you're back. I was so worried about you," Mary Lou whispered huskily.

Jade had forgotten all about her neighbour. She looked over at the slumped outline of the old woman. Mary Lou was wiping the perspiration off her face with the sleeve of her cardigan. She was holding the torch but her shaking hand made the light hop erratically around the attic. Jade could see the skeletal shape of her bones from her hips to her feet, as her damp pants clung tightly to her legs.

Mary Lou's peculiar odour drifted over to Jade. A mixture of rose water, camphor, sweat and old skin. It was even stronger than the dusty dried-wood smell peculiar to the attic. Jade's stomach heaved. She wanted to run away from the old woman, the smell, the rising water and the burning heat of the attic. But there was nowhere for her to go. Like Grandma and Mary Lou, she was now cut off from escaping.

The sound of lapping, sucking water mocked her. The horror of it all wrapped itself around her like a dark shroud.

"We can't stay here. I wanna die," Mary Lou whimpered.

VII
A Nightmare

"I'm gonna faint." The words dashed out of Jade's mouth. She wanted Grandma to ignore Mary Lou, pull her into her arms and tell her that this was all a bad dream.

Grandma was busy tearing the large towels into pieces, the size of small facecloths. She poured drinking water out of one bottle onto one of the pieces and handed it to Mary Lou, saying, "This'll help cool you, Miss Mary Lou."

Then she poured water onto another piece of towel. Pulling Jade close to her bosom, she gently wiped the grimy sweat off her face, saying in a no-nonsense but kindly voice, "My baby's gonna be strong now."

This commanded Jade's attention. It pulled the weakness and self-pity over her head. Like the way

Grandma used to take her sweater off when she was little – holding her close while tightly pulling it, gently but firmly, over her ears and head until it was finally off.

"We haven't had any breakfast! Help me find the cereal, Jade. I shoved it into the top o' one o' the bags."

"Will we have to eat it dry, Grandma?"

"Guess so. There's a few oranges in the bag with the cereal. I just grabbed them before we left. We've a few small bottles of water, too."

Grandma, Jade and Mary Lou, lathered in sweat, began to eat fistfuls of cereal, sitting on boxes in the airless attic. Jade knew the temperature had to be over a hundred degrees. She reached for a small bottle of water, put it to her mouth and gulped it down. She was filling it again from one of the big bottles when she heard an odd sound.

"What's that bangin', Bernice?" Mary Lou had cocked her ear towards the attic opening.

Jade jumped up to look down the hole where the ladder rested. She was shocked to find the water halfway up the ladder. Climbing down, she could see the sofa and chairs banging into the walls and doors as the angry, rough water continued to rush into the house, lifting every movable thing on its tidal surge.

Jade caught sight of the fridge floating on its side in the water.

"The fridge's floatin', Grandma! Things floatin' 'n' bangin' into each other," Jade yelled.

When she climbed back up again, terror gripped her. She felt paralysed, unable to move. Every fibre in her body urged her to scream for help. *But what good will that do? Who would hear a scream from the attic? The three of us are gonna die! We'll suffocate or drown and no one will know.*

Jade wanted so desperately to run away from this flood, from the attic, from Mary Lou – and even from Grandma.

"Grandma we must get outta here," Jade whispered, her mouth filled with choking dust.

"We'll wait a couple o' hours, Baby. By then, the water should be gone down again," Grandma said, taking the end of her T-shirt to wipe the perspiration off her face.

"We'll be dead in a couple o' hours, Grandma," Jade said in a mournful whisper from her position on the floor. She drew her knees up close. Hugging them, she lay her head gently on them.

Grandma began to peel the skin off one of the oranges. Jade didn't know that something as ordinary as peeling and sectioning an orange could be so calming. An orange had such a beautiful, fresh smell. She took some of the skin out of Grandma's hand and squeezed it between her fingers, rubbing it on her face and hands. Then she slowly put a juicy segment into her mouth, running the orange flavour all over her teeth with her tongue, to make it last as long as possible.

Closing her eyes for a moment, she recalled that the day was Monday. *This should be a normal school day.* She imagined herself sitting in the cafeteria beside Natasha. Usually her friend could only eat half an orange after lunch. Jade always ate Natasha's half as well as her own.

What's Natasha doin' now? And my other school friends? David Seemore? Was he right about the levees?

As if she knew what Jade was thinking, Mary Lou said, "Bernice, do you think we could find out about the levees on WWL? I have a radio in my bag."

She lifted her big black bag onto her lap and rummaged inside. Finally, she took out a small blue battery-operated radio.

Grandma took the radio and tried to tune in to a station. It crackled and whined. She pulled out the antenna and turned it this way and that.

Is the interference because we're in an attic? Jade wondered.

Finally, Grandma found a station. Jade could barely hear a man's voice saying, "Hurricane Katrina . . . landfall . . . East of New Orleans . . . this morning . . . 135 miles per hour winds. Alarming news . . . levees . . . breached . . . New Orleans. Floodwater . . . six to eight feet deep . . ."

"FLOODS! WHAT'S GOIN' TO HAPPEN TO US? WE'LL DROWN! WE'LL DROWN!" Jade screamed as if she was going mad with terror.

Grandma was staring at the radio as if it had cast a spell on her, turning her into a block of ice, silent and immobile. Jade crumpled down on the floor, pulling her knees up tightly to her body and wrapping her arms around them. She was frozen in time. Mary Lou began to whine, "Oh God, let me die now," and rocked back and forth making plaintive little sounds, "uh . . . uh . . . uh . . . uh . . . uh."

Grandma listened to the entire news bulletin before switching off the radio and handing it back to Mary Lou who took it from her as if in another world. Jade could see terror in Grandma's eyes as she jumped to her feet. Perspiration was running down her face and neck making a big dark V on the front of her T-shirt.

"Where's the axe, Jade?" Grandma shouted as she used her torch to make a sweeping arc around the sides of the attic.

Jade had seen the axe the time she had gone into the attic looking for Grandma's suitcase. "Why do you keep an axe in the attic, Grandma?" she had asked then.

"If the levees break in a hurricane and the floodwaters rise, we can only go up. On the roof."

"Grandma, how could you stay on a roof with no shade – in the bakin' summer heat of N'Awlins?" Jade had asked. "You'd die of sun stroke."

Grandma had answered then, "Baby, desperation makes you do desperate things in life."

Jade remembered where the axe was. She sprang up and pushed past Mary Lou to get it from the corner near her.

Grandma grabbed the axe from her and attacked the shingles at the lower end of the sloping roof, opposite where Mary Lou sat huddled. Jade could see the determination in the angle of Grandma's jaw and in her clenched teeth. She felt an urgency with every bang. When Grandma paused to wipe the stinging perspiration out of her eyes with a piece of dampened towel, Jade snatched the axe and swung it at the spot where a tiny point of light could be seen.

"Good girl, Jade. You're doin' a great job," Mary Lou said, her voice barely above a whisper.

A big shingle broke away, falling to the outside.

Jade kept swinging the axe with all her strength. She kept widening the hole until she believed it was large enough for Grandma to get through.

"That's big enough, Baby. Take a rest now."

Jade was exhausted. She was panting for breath. Her tongue was sticking to the top of her mouth. She could see the grey sky and feel fresh air coming into the stifling, hot-as-hell attic. *Maybe we'd be better off to stay in the attic, waitin' for the water to go down, than to go out on a slopin' roof with no shade*, she thought.

"We need to get out on the roof to be rescued," Grandma said, putting an end to Jade's thoughts about staying where they were.

"Bernice, you can leave me here to die. I'll only be a nuisance," Mary Lou whispered breathlessly. She feebly rubbed her face and neck with the damp cloth and took deep, audible sighs.

"No way, Miss Mary Lou. The three of us'll stick together. Where one goes, all three go."

Jade began to feel sorry for Grandma's friend. She had to admit to herself that Mary Lou had been very kind to her many times when Grandma had to work late in the restaurant. *It must be terrible to be old and feeble now when life has become hell*, Jade thought.

"We've no time to lose," Grandma's quick actions matched her words. She dragged two wooden crates from the corner, dumped their contents on the floor, pouncing on a fresh discovery as she did so.

"This extension cord might come in handy," she said as she began to loop a long orange electric cord around her elbow and hand. She put the freshly formed coil into her large brown holdall. Then she lifted one of the crates to place it directly below the hole in the roof.

"Jade, be ready to hold Miss Mary Lou's hand. Be careful in helpin' her through the hole."

Mary Lou got up stiffly and shuffled over to the crate holding her big black bag.

"Here, Miss Mary Lou, let me hold that for you. Let Jade get out on the roof first," Grandma said taking the big black bag out of Mary Lou's hand and putting it on the floor beside her.

Jade got up on the crate and pulled herself through the hole by leaning on her hands and arms. Once out on the roof, the wind and rain fell fresh on her body and were a welcome relief from the suffocating heat in the attic.

It was when she tried to stand up that she had difficulty. A sudden gust of wind blew the rain like a thousand tiny knives cutting into her skin. She felt the wind would lift her up, like Grandma said, and throw her into the mucky water that was lapping around the house. Her teeth chattering with nerves and the terror in her heart pulling the roof of her mouth downwards, she forced out a long, thin scream, "Grandmaaaaaaaaaa. Heeeeeelp."

It was then she heard the other screams. Muffled screams from the attics of houses nearby and piercing screams from the rooftops. These screams rose higher than the wind and were more terrifying.

I must be gonna die, Jade thought.

The wind was locking her knees together. She struggled to lower her body down slowly, to crouch on the roof close to the hole. All around she could see water, water, water: blackish-brown, putrid water swirling around their house, high enough to lick at the gutters.

She shuddered to think that their neighbourhood was now a big dark lake, infested with snakes and alligators. *Louisiana is mostly swampland and snakes ride the high water*, she thought. She recalled how Grandma had told her that Cottonmouth Water Moccasins – deadly poisonous snakes – had come up on the floodwaters in Houma during a storm. They were found inside trailers. There were so many, they had to be shot.

Natasha had seen alligators in the lake near her house. That thought petrified Jade and the odour of rotten trash, sewers and oil made her gag. Then she noticed people huddled together on the roof of a house about a block over. For a minute she forgot her own misery. She counted four adults and three children. Their screams sent a wild shiver all over Jade's skull and down her back.

"Help us! Save us! Pleeeeeeeeeease," they pleaded.

A cry began deep down in Jade's belly and forced itself up through her throat, only to die there in a pitiful, long squeak, "Grandmaaaaaaaaaa – I'm scared." She felt sick deep in her stomach. She was shaking all over.

Then Mary Lou's head appeared, followed slowly by her neck, shoulders and then her arm. Jade crouched on her knees near the hole to grab Mary Lou's bony hand. Grandma began pushing her from below.

"I . . . can't . . . do . . . it, . . . Ber . . . nee . . ." Mary Lou's voice trailed off into the hot air.

"Come on, Miss Mary Lou. Jade and I are here to help you."

Mary Lou gave a long low moan as Jade grabbed her hand and arm, pulling her upward while Grandma pushed from below. Finally, they were able to shove and heave her onto the roof. She curled herself into a ball and lay exhausted, close to the hole. Driving rain was soaking her flimsy clothes.

Jade crouched down beside the hole. Grandma

passed her big brown holdall, the food and the water through the hole to Jade. Then, she heaved herself up and wriggled onto the roof, where she lay for a few minutes near Jade and Mary Lou.

Suddenly, a piercing scream for help rent the air. It was quite near. Jade sat bolt upright and clung to Grandma as they both looked in the direction of the scream.

"My God, that house has moved off its foundation. Those people'll fall into the water. God have mercy on us," Grandma whispered as if anything louder might tip the balance.

Jade felt as if she had stepped inside a horror movie. One blood curdling thing after another was happening. *What can I do?* She looked at the long, orange extension cord Grandma was taking out of her bag. *Is Grandma goin' to throw it over to the people on top of the house?*

"What are you gonna do with that, Grandma?" Jade asked.

"We need to wrap this around the three of us and tie ourselves to the chimney. That way, no one'll get blown off the roof."

Jade stared at Grandma in disbelief. *WHAT! We'll be tied together on a roof. Surely this is a bad dream. A nightmare!*

"Here, Jade, put this end around your waist and hold it," Grandma ordered, handing her the end of the extension cord that plugged into the outlet. Jade fingered its three hard prongs before winding the cord around her waist. Grandma moved Mary Lou closer before passing it around her. Jade felt like a frog that curious boys had trapped in a jam jar.

"I hate this, Grandma," she shouted grouchily between clenched teeth.

"She's doin' what's best for us, Jade," Mary Lou said in a gentle, persuasive voice.

"Let's get closer to the chimney," Grandma said ignoring what Jade had just said. She directed Jade and Mary Lou to sit down before she secured the cord to the chimney and to herself and passed it back to Jade. Once seated, she then helped Jade to tie it with a knot.

Although the blazing sun reflected off the roof and the water, its brightness did nothing to lift the dark mood that was binding Jade. She slouched down inside the electric cord, complaining to herself that it wasn't fair. Feeling her legs burning on the roof tiles, she wanted to scream, but knowing that Grandma wouldn't like it and Mary Lou would side with Grandma, she began to sulk.

After a long time feeling sorry for herself, with no

words being spoken between the three of them, Jade told herself that this nightmare wouldn't last. *In fact, I'll wake up after a night's sleep and everything'll be the way it was before the hurricane.*

VIII
Tied to a Chimney

The electric cord around their waists bound Jade, Grandma and Mary Lou to each other and to the chimney on the roof.

Their house was now an island among many islands in a debris-strewn lake with dirty water lapping angrily at the gutters.

Jade's heart felt as if it had moved up her chest to sit just behind the back of her throat, making her feel so tight she could hardly breathe.

The constant screams from attics and rooftops made her insides feel like a snake pit.

She held the extension cord out from her body as far as she could.

It is so hot! With her body so close to Grandma's, Jade felt she was in a furnace. Her clothes were damp with sweat and sticking to her skin. Wriggling to make a little space between Grandma and herself, she slipped down to where the electric cord was now under her arm pits.

Jade looked up at the sky to take her mind off what was happening on the roof. The rain had stopped and the clouds were breaking up and drifting away in fine wisps. The sun gradually became a big, blazing ball of light overhead. Soon Jade had to shade her eyes and look away. She welcomed the sun's heat for drying her rain-drenched clothes but then it began to burn her scalp and skin.

Mary Lou's quivery, light voice broke into Jade's thoughts, "You're getting more like your Mama, Jade. I remember when she was your age. She was always kind to me. I used to mind Keisha every day after school for your Grandma when she worked in Zack's restaurant from twelve to seven."

Jade was embarrassed to hear Mary Lou talking about her Mama. *How much does the old woman know about her?* Nevertheless, she still wanted her elderly neighbour to talk about the mother she never knew.

"I'm glad my Mama . . . helped you, Miss Mary Lou."

Jade often wondered how her Mama really looked. She had a couple of pictures of her that were taken in grade school but none of her as a young woman. She asked the burning question, "Do I look like her?" Jade held her breath waiting to hear what Mary Lou would say.

"Yeah. You're a lot like her. Isn't she, Bernice?"

"Yeah, I suppose so."

Grandma didn't say anything else. Jade knew that Grandma never talked about her Mama. Probably Mary Lou didn't know that.

Heaving herself up a bit nearer the chimney and the others, Grandma said matter of factly, "Now the three of us must help each other. No matter what happens, the three of us must stick together."

* * *

Jade looked at the front of her house where the road should be. There was no road. Only a lake. The few oak trees still standing on Seventh Oak Street looked like large shrubs above the water. Their trunks well hidden under the brown, swirling lake. Their top branches full of all kinds of debris.

Then Jade saw a terrible sight. Two houses had crashed into each other. The wind and water had pushed them off their foundation slabs.

She had a completely new thought. *Only the President of the United States can help us now.*

Looking up into Grandma's face, Jade asked the question that she believed was somehow an answer, "Grandma, the President will rescue us, won't he?"

"I'm sure he'll send help, Baby," was her reply, but it didn't allay Jade's fears.

Grandma must have known how afraid she was because she put her arm around Jade's shoulders and said, "Remember when the Israelites were wanderin' in the desert? They depended on God for everything and God led them out of their slavery."

Giving her a tight hug Grandma lowered her head and whispered into Jade's ear, "God'll rescue us, Baby. We must keep the faith."

Jade remembered that story from the Bible. But when she recalled that the Israelites were wandering for forty years, she asked Grandma, "How long will God allow us to be on this roof before we get rescued?"

"We'll be rescued soon, Jade. We gotta keep believin'."

Jade snuggled into Grandma. She needed her strength.

* * *

Time was now trapped in a watery grave.

Eventually Jade fell asleep. She dreamed she was ordering people to throw coals and branches of trees on a large fire. Great flames were twisting and leaping high and the branches crackled and sparked. The screams for help were terrifying.

When she opened her eyes, she was relieved to see no flames – but heart-rending screams still pierced her eardrums.

She looked over to see where the screams were coming from. A big two-storey house had split in two and people who had been on the roof were now clinging desperately to the gutters.

As Jade watched in horror, a woman, who had slipped off the broken roof, could no longer hold on to her husband's hand and fell with a scream into the water. The piercing screech of the woman shot through Jade's body like a laser beam, reaching her heart and freezing it in a nanosecond.

When her heart thawed a little, thoughts somersaulted through her mind: *What will become of the woman? Did she drown quickly or were there snakes and alligators lurkin' under the surface of the water lookin' for food?*

A deep shudder began at Jade's toes, ran up her legs and around the rest of her body, making her shake all over. Wanting to vomit, she retched and retched but nothing came up. Grandma held her hand over Jade's forehead to help her but still she couldn't vomit.

Then Grandma poured some of the precious drinking water on her piece of towel and wiped Jade's clammy brow with it. Putting it on top of her granddaughter's head to shade her from the scorching sun, she said gently, "Baby, don't take it so hard."

Pain was written in her eyes and on her kind brown face. She pulled Jade close to her, wrapping her arms around her to shield her from the harshness of this tragedy.

Mary Lou remained silent.

Freeing one arm from Jade, Grandma put it around her friend's shoulders and murmured, "God have mercy. Lord help us."

Mary Lou and Jade stayed with Grandma's arms around them for some time.

Jade's body began to calm down.

In the midst of this hell, she stopped feeling bad about being tied to Grandma and Mary Lou. At least for now, they were safe.

* * *

When she was sitting there, baking in the heat with nothing to do, Jade thought of dialling Natasha's cell phone.

She was shocked and excited when her friend answered. Natasha's voice sounded tiny and strained. Jade's usual warm feeling gave way to anxiety, "Natasha, it's Jade. Where are you? Did you evacuate?"

"Hi, Jade, I'm at home. We didn't evacuate. We're all upstairs. The water's up to the veranda near the bedroom."

"Oh, God, Natasha. Did your cousins come over before the storm?"

"Yeah, Melanie, Trudy and Tyler came, and my aunt and uncle. They're all here. Where are you, Jade?"

"We're tied to the chimney on the roof," Jade said, feeling as if she was playing the part of the heroine in a play and not feeling like herself. *Weird.*

"Oh, my God! I'm terrified. Are you? You should see the alligators and sn—"

The phone went dead.

Jade held the phone in disbelief. Natasha was gone. *Alligators and snakes!* She shuddered as she tried Natasha's number again but the strange whirring sound was not a line. Jade felt so empty.

Natasha was just like her, stuck in a flood. Jade didn't want to admit to herself that she felt a bit better when she heard that Natasha was stuck too.

"How's Natasha and her family doin'?" Grandma asked quietly.

When Jade told Grandma that the floodwater was up to the veranda on the second floor she said, "They're lucky they have an upstairs. I hope they keep safe, Baby."

Jade hoped they'd keep safe too. She couldn't get Natasha out of her mind. She thought about Natasha's mama and daddy and her mischievous little brother, Kyle, whom Natasha adored. *It would have been so good to have visited them for a swim and a barbecue but the hurricane cancelled those plans. Now Natasha is just like me – stuck in a flood.*

Grandma's phone rang.

It was Auntie Lynn.

Grandma's voice quivered as she told Lynn that they were tied together on the roof. Lynn must have been hysterical on the other end because Jade saw Grandma wiping the tears from her eyes with her free hand.

Jade got the gist of the conversation from the way Grandma kept repeating the most shocking bits – almost as if by saying them over it helped her to get her head around what was happening to them all.

Grandma asked Lynn how she and the boys were doing. Then she said, her voice shaking, "Lynn, try to get us help."

After she'd said goodbye, she put the phone back into her pocket and wiped her tears with the back of her hand. Blinking the remaining tears away and giving a little shake she said, "We'd better eat."

She took a packet of crackers and a can of tuna out of one of the food bags. In her big brown bag she found a spoon and began to put some tuna on the crackers.

The smell of tuna stinks with all the other fishy, oily and sewer smells. Jade screwed her face up in disgust. She just knew she couldn't touch the tuna.

Mary Lou wasn't hungry either but Grandma insisted they eat, "We must keep up our strength. Close your eyes and don't think about smells."

Then she gave each of them a small bottle of water saying, "We must drink. We don't wanna get dehydrated."

By the time Jade had finished nibbling tuna and crackers, the last colour was fading from the sky. Little points of light flashed as people on the rooftops and in the attics shone their torches into the darkness in frantic pleas for help.

Jade was reminded of Halloween as she looked out at the derelict houses. But Halloween was make-believe. Scary fun. This was for real and it was a different kind of being terrified.

* * *

Night-time on Monday brought an eerie silence to the neighbourhood. Even the screams and the barking and yelping of dogs stopped. It was as if all living things folded into the darkness with the growing realisation that they would not be rescued. They all shared the misery of feeling abandoned.

The only sound to be heard was the water lapping at the gutters of the houses.

Jade lay down with her arms over the electrical cord. Her eyes were shut tight but she could still see the brownish-black lake around her house and smell the stench of sewers and rotting trash.

Then, through her shut eyelids, she saw something bright. She opened her eyes just as she heard the sound of a helicopter high overhead. An arc of light swept over the water, making a grey glow on its surface. It stopped for a minute at the chimney.

"Grandma, they're comin' to rescue us," Jade shouted excitedly, thinking what fun it would be to travel in a helicopter.

"I hope so," Grandma said pulling herself to an upright position.

"They're only looking," Mary Lou murmured in a sad voice as the arc of light left them and the sound of the helicopter faded away in the distance.

Jade couldn't believe it. She burrowed deeply into

Grandma again and hid her head under her arm. Her heart ached for comfort and reassurance.

After a while she pushed the electric cord down to her waist again, pulled herself into a sitting position, wiped her eyes on Grandma's shoulder and rested her head there.

She stayed resting on Grandma until she fell asleep in the early hours of Tuesday.

IX
Room for One

A nightmare is only a dream. At the worst part of the dream, you wake up. Then you feel relieved that you're back to normal.

Jade did not wake up and find life back to normal. What she was experiencing in real life was worse than a nightmare.

When she woke up on Tuesday morning she was still pressed up against Grandma. Her clothes were soaking wet with perspiration. She was still tied to Grandma and Mary Lou on the roof.

Mary Lou was moaning, "Bernice, I'm not gonna make it. My back sore."

"Of course, you'll make it, Miss Mary Lou. Let me rub your back."

When Grandma stretched to rub her friend's back, the

electric cord tightened around Jade's waist. She wanted to squeal but she knew Grandma wouldn't like it.

The sun was shining with a feeble, watery light over the wreck of their neighbourhood. In the tight strangeness, Jade did not feel like herself. She was tired being tied to Grandma and Mary Lou, so she began to wriggle underneath the electric cord.

Noticing this, Grandma said, "You hungry, Baby? There's bread and chips in your bag. Put the chips between the slices 'n' it'll give a flavour. We still have plenty o' water."

Jade pulled the bag containing the bread towards her, took out two slices and put cheese and onion potato chips between them as Grandma had suggested. She had just finished the dry sandwich when she first heard the distant rumble. Then the sound seemed to come closer, fade and come again.

"Sounds like a helicopter," Mary Lou said as she slowly drank some water. "Sure hope they see us," she added wistfully.

Jade squinted up at the sky, looking for the first sight of the helicopter. Its deep throbbing was growing louder, assuring her that it was heading in their general direction.

"Baby, wave your T-shirt," Grandma told Jade as she rummaged in her big brown bag.

"Grandma, they did come back for us. I knew they would," Jade shouted with excitement. "I'd love to take a ride in a helicopter."

"There's a mirror here somewhere," Grandma murmured.

On finding a small, round mirror she told her granddaughter, "Baby, gimme the T-shirt. Try to get the sun to shine in the mirror. That'll cause a big flash. It'll show 'em where we are."

Taking the mirror, Jade jiggled it up and down until it caught the sun's light and flashed. *This is fun*, she thought, as she gave it her complete attention.

When the helicopter came into view in the distance, a huge bird lurching towards them, its rotary blades scissoring the bright sky, Jade pointed the flashing mirror in its direction.

Grandma waved the T-shirt and Jade screamed at the top of her voice behind the mirror.

"I can't WAIT to ride in a helicopter," Jade shrieked.

"Baby, take it easy. That electric cord bitin' into me," Grandma said with annoyance.

"Grandma, it's comin' towards us," Jade shouted above the increasing noise as she eased down again beside her grandmother.

The noise from the helicopter was now deafening.

Jade was forced to clap one hand over her ear, while holding the mirror in the other. The wind generated by the giant propellers forced Jade to bore into Grandma's side for protection. She was so nervous her hand wobbled holding the mirror. She wanted to jump up and yet she had to try to keep the mirror at the correct angle to reflect the sun. *It's all soooo hard. I have to get it right*, Jade thought. *This may be our only chance of being rescued.*

The helicopter stopped directly above the roof. It hovered there like a prehistoric bird with wings flapping straight up from its back in the vortex of a mighty wind. Jade's heart thumped so loudly she could hear it as well as the deafening noise of the helicopter. She continued to cling to Grandma for protection from the wind.

Shielding her eyes in order to be able to look up, she read, '**United States Coast Guard**'. A soldier was lowered down in a basket, stopping just above the chimney. He shouted down, "We've room for one person. What about the old woman?"

It seemed like eternity to Jade before Grandma spoke. In that long time, Jade thought that maybe she could be the one to be saved. She was young after all and in some rescue scenes she had seen in movies, the children were saved first. Her heart stopped beating.

"There are three of us here and where one goes, all three go," Grandma shouted back over the noise of the helicopter.

"Sorry, Ma'am, we don't have room for three. Just one."

"No. We're together. Where one goes, the three of us go," Grandma repeated, her jaw at that defiant angle Jade knew so well.

"Sorry. We have to leave you then, Ma'am."

Jade's mouth dropped open in one big gasp of disappointment. Her throat, her stomach and her head were now sore. She felt she was witnessing everything as if in an IMAX audience wearing 3-D glasses – bringing everything near – but not real. She watched the basket being drawn up into the helicopter again.

Was that our only chance of being rescued? Maybe the soldier will send another helicopter with room for three people?

Abandonment and fear gripped Jade. She slumped down inside the electric cord and when the helicopter turned around and flew behind their chimney and out of sight, Jade began to sink into nothing but terror. Nightmare terror.

The noise from the helicopter grew fainter until they could hear it no more. They were left behind in the most awful silence, tied together on a roof in the blazing sunshine, with no shade.

Jade could not get rid of a terrible feeling of emptiness. When she had felt empty in the past, she had called her friend Natasha. It worked yesterday. Natasha answered. But this time, when she rang the familiar number, she only heard a shrill whistle.

Terror grabbed Jade's heart and whispered into her ear, *You'll die – tied to Grandma and Mary Lou on a roof.*

She remembered Mr Cooper telling the class that you should breathe deeply when you feel a panic attack coming. He had demonstrated how to sit on a chair with your feet on the ground breathing in and out: *In 2,3,4,5. Out 2,3,4,5.*

Jade discovered that she couldn't breathe deeply, slumped down inside the electric cord, so she gently straightened herself up into a sitting position. She was careful not to put any pressure on the electric cord in case she hurt Grandma or Mary Lou. She began her deep breaths. Mr Cooper had taught her well. Slowly, she felt calmer.

*   *   *

Grandma and Mary Lou were dozing off and on. No one felt like talking in this terrible heat.

Jade kept looking out on the gigantic lake as far as she could see. Suddenly, she thought she saw something moving in the distance. She held her breath. She was nearly afraid to think it, *Is it a boat coming in our direction?*

Mr Cooper had told them one day in Geography class that people see mirages in the desert when they've been without water in the burning heat for some time. They imagine they see someone or something. Even though she wasn't in the desert, Jade was feeling very thirsty and she had been sitting for hours in the burning heat, like desert heat. *Is this a mirage?* Jade asked herself hesitantly.

She felt a big tug on the electric cord and Grandma began shouting and waving the T-shirt, "Please help us. Over here!"

A young man was rowing a small boat towards them. He shouted as he steered the boat parallel with the roof, "Would you like me to bring y'all to high ground?"

Although he said 'y'all' like New Orleans people, he said everything else in a strange accent.

Deep blue eyes stared at them from a thin freckled face with a long chin. A crop of red hair pushed its way out from under his Red Sox baseball cap.

"Will you be able to take the three of us?" Grandma asked.

"Yeah. Take your time."

"Stay here until I see," Grandma said, untying the electric cord from around her waist.

She inched her way down the sloping roof on her hands and knees with the big brown holdall on her back and dragging two plastic bags of food and water. Carefully she handed the bags, one by one, to the young man, who was leaning one of his oars into the corner of the roof gutter to anchor the boat in one place.

Then Grandma came back up the roof on all fours. Taking the cord off Mary Lou, she said to Jade, "Baby, come down behind Miss Mary Lou. Take a plastic bag and Miss Mary Lou's black bag. Put your knapsack on your back."

Taking the electric cord and wrapping it around her elbow and hand, she said, "This electric cord might come in handy again."

Grandma crawled back down with it and with Mary Lou directly behind her. Jade took up the rear. The asphalt scratched her knees, but she knew not to complain. There was no room for self-pity. When they reached the end of the roof, all three of them stood up gingerly, huddling close together, drawing strength from each other.

Handing the extension cord and the remaining bags to the young man, Grandma balanced herself on the roof near the gutter, saying, "Miss Mary Lou, you go first."

"Careful. Take it slowly," their rescuer urged as he stood, one foot stretched out in front of the other to keep his balance. While holding the oar firmly in the gutter, he extended his other hand to Mary Lou.

Her long nails were sticking into the palms of Jade's hand as she held her firmly. Now Grandma was asking Mary Lou to let go and step out into a boat that was bobbing about on filthy water. Jade held her breath as the old woman balanced on one thin leg. She had rolled up the bottoms of her trousers. Jade found it hard to look at her leg, which was covered in flaky, dry skin and had blue veins bulging out like playdough snakes.

Both Jade and Grandma gripped Mary Lou's hand and arm as she balanced precariously on one leg, until Grandma said, "Jade, you let go. This could be dangerous".

Mary Lou put her right leg into the boat hesitantly. The boat rocked a little. The man's strong hand helped her steady herself enough to bring her other leg into the boat. She let go of Grandma's hand and the boat rocked away from the roof as she brought her whole body in.

Once in the boat, she nestled her frail body against the young man's frame, like a bird with a broken wing finding shelter under a strong oak. Her rescuer led her gently to a seat on the boat before steering the boat back against the gutter again for Jade. She was trying to balance between the sloping end of the roof and the boat. Even with the greatest care, the boat bobbed up and down on the water and frightened Jade.

"Grandmaaaaaaaaaaaaaa!"

"You're alright, Baby. Take it easy," Grandma said in a reassuring voice.

As Jade lifted her right leg into the boat she thought she had missed the side as it lurched away from the roof. The man held her by the hand and elbow as the boat rocked from side to side, moving away again from the gutter.

Jade was shaking. The man led her down to sit opposite Mary Lou, who was doubled over, arms on knees, looking at the bottom of the boat.

Jade worried that Grandma's weight would capsize the boat when she stepped in. It was taking Grandma so long to take that step. Jade could see that she was very nervous, putting one foot out and then taking it back again.

"Come on Grandma! You can do it!" Jade urged.

Her voice sounded high-pitched in a way she did

not recognise as hers but her words of encouragement seemed to work. Grandma held out her hand to the man and stepped off the roof into the boat. It gave a big lurch to one side, causing Jade to fall on top of Mary Lou's weak, frail body.

"Oh, God!" the old woman prayed, "Keep us safe."

When Grandma was seated opposite her in the boat, Jade was able to breathe a little more freely.

The boatman leaned on the oar to push against the gutter. Slowly they pulled away from the roof.

Perspiration was sitting on Grandma's brow in large beads that gathered and then broke away quickly in watery lines on her wet, dark face. She was breathing in quick, shallow gulps, running her tongue along her upper lip to catch the perspiration. Then taking the end of her T-shirt, she bent over, drawing it along her forehead and over her face.

Jade had never seen Grandma so stressed before. She got up out of her place and gingerly stepped over to sit beside her. Putting her arm around Grandma's waist, she rested her head on her shoulder saying, "It's alright, Grandma. We're safe now."

Grandma began to relax and breathe normally.

The young man steered the boat out into the dank water. He spoke with a clipped, flat accent, "Hi, folks. My name's Brad. I'm originally from Boston. I came down here on a visit years ago and fell in love with this place, so I stayed."

Brad wanted to talk. He told Grandma, Mary Lou and Jade that he had to take out his boat once he realised that people were trapped in attics and on roofs by the floodwater.

"This journey's been so treacherous. I had to come very slowly. Under the deep water, there's piles of debris, stop signs, submerged cars and spewing gas lines. It's dangerous, I tell ye."

Then Jade caught sight of it – the body of a black man lying face down in the water, his arms open wide at his side. She had seen people sky-diving on TV with their arms stretched out like that, the air ballooning their clothes. This was different. This man was dead. Drowned.

Jade began to shudder uncontrollably. Grandma grabbed her, pulling her close.

"Yeah. It's terrible," Brad said. "We can't do anything about the dead. Sad. Too many people to be rescued."

He slowed down and steered the boat in a big arc past the corpse.

They continued on for some time without speaking. The journey was like something out of a horror movie. Suddenly Brad broke the deathly silence. Smiling at Mary Lou, he said, "Ma'am you remind me of my great aunt."

Then he gave a nervous laugh and said, "Can you believe her name is Katrina? She's a real lady."

Jade could only think of one thing – the hurricane – when she heard the name Katrina. As if he understood how she was feeling, Brad said, "Umph, this Katrina ain't no lady."

"Oh, look at that man in the tree," Jade said, pointing to a man, who was standing on a branch and clinging to the trunk of an oak tree. It was easy now to see the top of the tree because the water was up so high. The man seemed to be so relieved to see the boat that Jade was afraid he'd do something foolish, like jump in and capsize it.

Brad brought the boat close to the tree and said, "Slowly. Careful, man. Take it easy. Slowly, slowly."

He had trouble keeping the boat from lurching away from the tree so he said to the man, "Slide down as slowly and gently as you can. Be ready when I come close to the tree."

Then Grandma had an idea, "What about throwing the extension cord around that branch to anchor the boat?"

"That'll do it," Brad said as he grabbed the cord from the bottom of the boat. He made a large knot threw it around a strong branch. He pulled tightly on the cord to secure it.

The man slid down from the tree into the boat. It rocked from side to side. Jade thought it was going to capsize and she screamed, "Grandmaaaaaaaaaaaaaaa!"

Grandma pulled her close again as she always did when Jade screamed her name.

The man sat down beside Mary Lou. His dirty and torn blue shirt hung over wet khaki shorts. He had nothing on his feet.

Jade couldn't stop staring at the man's face. Grandma had always said it was bad manners to stare, but she couldn't help it. The stranger was covered in red bumps all over his brown face, neck, arms and legs.

He took big long gasps of air. He had no words until Grandma gave him a long drink.

"I climbed . . . up a tree . . . when the water . . . came up . . . so quickly," he whispered hesitantly. "I didn't know how to swim – so I was trapped – in the tree. The fire ants were the worst."

That's what caused the bumps, Jade thought.

Grandma poured some water onto a piece of towel and gave it to the man to cool the burning in his face. He nodded his thanks.

This has to be hell, Jade thought. *So much suffering. Everybody has a terrible story to tell. It will never end.*

She closed her eyes to get away from all of the pain, but her imagination created ants the size of house flies and she could see them crawling all over the man. There was no escape from the horror of it all. She shuddered.

"Where are we going now?" Mary Lou asked Brad when he had coiled up the electric cord and pushed off again.

"I'll bring you to high ground and then go back for others," the Good Samaritan said.

It wasn't too long before they reached an elevated expressway, a bridge rising out of the mucky water. Brad eased the boat over to the top of the ramp. He jumped out and moored the boat to the guardrail with the electric cord. This made it much easier for Grandma, Mary Lou, Jade and the strange man to climb out.

"I sure hope you get some help here," Brad said as he helped each of them out of the boat.

Jade staggered to get her balance on the cement. Being tied for so long on the roof and then sitting in a cramped boat had left her feeling unsteady on her feet.

She watched the strange man drifting away from them, ghost-like, into the throng of lost-looking people on the bridge. As he approached a group of dishevelled men who were passing around a bottle of whiskey, they called out, "Come on, bro'."

One man pushed over to make room for him and offered him the bottle, which he quickly put to his head before another man grabbed it off him.

"We'll go over here, Jade," Grandma said, tugging her granddaughter's arm as she struggled with plastic bags, her big holdall, Mary Lou's big black bag and Mary Lou.

Jade straightened her knapsack on her back, took two bags off Grandma and let Mary Lou link her as the three of them made their way over to a space near the guardrail on the other side of the bridge. There they sat on a narrow ledge until they were so uncomfortable that they had to slide down on the burning hot cement.

Jade couldn't stop an anxious feeling tighten her chest. It made her heart knock loudly. She remembered it was Tuesday.

The shadows of the rooftops were lengthening on the water.

"Will anyone rescue us? How long will we have to stay here?" she asked Grandma and Mary Lou.

"We have to be very patient 'n' keep the faith," Grandma replied.

Mary Lou nodded in agreement.

X

The Bridge to Nowhere

Jade clearly saw that they had been left on a bridge to nowhere. It rose up from swirling, brown, smelly water and stretched over the water as far as she could see.

From the bridge, the roofs of houses looked like rectangular lily-pads in a large dark lake. Telephone poles had been snapped in half. Sections of roofs were missing or trees had collapsed on them.

Thousands of birds were speckling the sky, shrieking their nervousness and loss of the familiar. They added to the eeriness Jade was feeling.

People were swarming over what had once been a busy highway. Some had been brought there by boat. Many had waded chest-deep to high ground through filthy water. Most had vague, traumatised looks. Some were so weak they couldn't stand. They huddled dejectedly in small groups getting support from each other. Men, women and children.

Jade noticed one woman who was much older than Grandma. She was wearing a flower-print dress and was walking with a cane because her ankles were swollen. A rag on her balding head protected her from the rays of the sun. She seemed to be leading a small group of family members. Their dead, dark eyes were full of pain and they looked as if they had been shocked into silence.

"I'm gonna look around to see if there's anything we can use to lie on," Grandma said as she got up slowly from the hot ground.

"My gums are sore, Jade," Mary Lou whispered.

"I'll stay with Miss Mary Lou," Jade said, noticing how much frailer the old woman looked without her teeth. She hadn't noticed until that moment that Mary Lou had removed them.

"Give Miss Mary Lou some o' your water for her gums, Jade," Grandma urged. "I'll be back in a few minutes."

Some people on the bridge kept asking over and over, "Does anyone know where we'll be goin'?"

Others said they heard that the Superdome had opened as a shelter. They said they wouldn't go there as the toilets were overflowing. The stench was terrible. The electricity had failed.

When Grandma returned with some cardboard and a small blanket she told Jade and Mary Lou what an old toothless man had told her, "The Superdome's leakin'. The winds punched holes in the roof."

"That's meant to be a shelter. We can't go there," Mary Lou said, her sunken mouth adding to her worried look.

Jade thought about the Superdome. It was one of the biggest indoor stadiums in the whole of the United States. She had gone there with Uncle Jordan to see the Saints playing the Cowboys. There were 75,000 people in the stadium watching the game that day. She remembered that the roof seemed to be made of white cement and had no windows. It was hard to believe that hurricane winds had damaged it.

Jade began to be afraid of some of the people around them. They were pacing up and down, shouting in anger about being abandoned.

The bridge was solid and their chances of being rescued were better but she had felt safer tied to Grandma and Mary Lou on the roof.

"This is the Red Sea – that's what we're trying to cross," an elderly man said to no one in particular.

Another man started shouting with the voice of a preacher, "This is a mass exodus like the Israelites fleeing Egypt to go to the Promised Land."

Grandma fixed the blanket on the cardboard for Mary Lou to lie on. Jade huddled close to them.

Then the screams began. The wild desperate pleas of people who had no food or drink and who had become delirious with the sun. They could see no Promised Land.

Jade was awash with fear, "Grandma, this is hell, isn't it? These are the screams of people in hell."

Then she added mournfully, "We've tried to be good, Grandma. Why is God punishing us?"

"Don't talk like that, Baby. God is a good God. He knows what we need. He'll look after us."

As if on cue, in the midst of the chaos, a woman's voice rose up in song. A beacon of light began to shine in the darkness. A small brown-skinned woman, her face full of pain, raised her big voice to the heavens. It came from deep down in her belly and resonated through every fibre of her being. She closed her eyes and sang out a gospel song to God.

She fanned into flames the tiny embers of faith in the souls of her long-suffering brothers and sisters:

> When this world is tossing me
> Like a ship on a raging sea
> Thou who rulest the wind and water
> Stand by me, stand by me . . .

Jade got up and moved closer to the woman. She stood with the people. They began to clap to the beat and sing out the words of the old Negro spiritual. Jade recalled Grandma telling her many times that her people had been comforted in their sufferings during slavery by singing spirituals. Now on this bridge to nowhere, she looked around the faces of the people singing. Many had their eyes closed and were singing with all their heart. Singing was helping them to forget their cares for a short while.

Peace fell like a warm blanket on Jade's shoulders. She recalled the distinctive smell of polished wood and lilies in Abyssinia Baptist Church which she attended every Sunday with Grandma.

When the brown-skinned woman's song was done, Grandma began to sing out in the deep, gravelly voice Jade had heard so often when she led the church choir:

> There is a balm in Gilead,
> To make the wounded whole . . .

A swell of song rose from the suffering people on the bridge. They sang with all of the emotion in their battered hearts. And they were calm for some time after silence fell.

Grandma helped Mary Lou to get comfortable before Jade and she lay down for the night. There wasn't any privacy. The guardrail was their bedroom wall and the sky their ceiling.

Sleep came slowly on the bridge to nowhere.

*   *   *

It was very hard to stay around Mary Lou and Grandma all of the time.

The next day, Jade wandered off to the far side of the bridge, drifting in and out of clusters of people, listening to bits of conversations and piecing together some of the happenings of the last couple of days. She learned that some people had looted stores after the hurricane. They had stolen everything from useless appliances to food and even liquor. In fact, she found a bottle of unopened Jameson whiskey propped up against the guardrail. Looking around, she saw the man who had been talking about crossing the Red Sea and offered it to him, asking for bread and water instead. He was delighted and gave her bread, water and a lump of cheese.

"Look what I have, Grandma," she announced when she returned to their place near the guardrail, proudly showing Grandma the bread, cheese and water.

"Your Grandma raised no dumb baby!" Grandma said with a big wide smile of satisfaction as she took the food and water from Jade.

Jade noticed that Mary Lou was still lying down near the guardrail. Her lips were dry and had begun to crack. Grandma carefully soaked the bread in some water before placing it in Mary Lou's mouth.

"Here, Miss Mary Lou, take a drink," Jade urged her as she raised the bottle of water to the old woman's dry lips.

Mary Lou sipped the water, murmuring her thanks before closing her eyes. She retreated again from the horror of it all into a fitful sleep.

When Jade had finished her bread, cheese and water ration, she went wandering around again. Her attention was drawn to a man who was balancing precariously on top of the guardrail. She began to shiver with fear. *He might fall backwards into the putrid water*, she thought.

A small crowd gathered around him. She heard him shout, "Isn't this America, the land of the free? Dr Martin Luther King won our freedom for us. Why are we not free now? Why are we forgotten? Why we gettin' no help?"

When people got agitated and shouted back, he slowly climbed down, wiped the perspiration from his face and sat down despondently on the ground.

Jade felt so sad and helpless. She thought it would be better to return to her own spot and the safety of her Grandma.

No one came to rescue the people off the bridge so Grandma, Mary Lou and Jade spent Wednesday night as well propped up against the guardrail. The air was stinking as the water swirled around them. People cried, moaned and shouted all through the night.

"Bernice, I'm done. I don't think I'll make it," Mary Lou winced with pain as she tried to turn over on the old piece of cardboard.

Grandma took a sweater out of her bag and rolling it in a ball, pushed it gently under the old woman's head, saying, "Miss Mary Lou, we can't go on without you! You'll make it. God's good."

Jade felt so sorry for her old neighbour. She thought about the last time she was in her house when Mary Lou had fixed her a sandwich. Then she prayed, *God, please help Miss Mary Lou to make it.*

Thinking that she might have something in her knapsack to help her neighbour pass the time, Jade found her MP3 player. *Maybe Mary Lou would like to listen to some music*, she thought. Then she remembered Mary Lou asking her once how she listened to 'that noise.'

Pulling out her shorts and tops, Jade rolled them into a neat ball and, gently holding up the old woman's head, she eased them under her neck saying, "Miss Mary Lou, see if this helps you to be more comfortable."

"Thanks, Honey," Mary Lou whispered, her mouth sunken, her lips dry, her eyes opening in narrow slits to look at Jade before she closed them again.

Grandma was sitting with her back against the guardrail. She had been observing Jade helping her friend. "Come here, Baby," she urged, holding out her arms.

Jade was glad to slip down on the ground beside her, feeling her warm embrace. Shortly after that, Jade began to doze, lying up against Grandma. She dreamed she was flying free, up above the clouds. For a short time she escaped the torment that was now her life.

XI
A New Friend

Jade had slept for three nights in the same clothes that she had been wearing when she climbed into the attic as the floodwaters rose after the hurricane. She used to fuss when Grandma made her shower every evening before going to bed, especially when she was watching her favourite programme on TV. This morning, Thursday, she would give anything for clean water to wash over her hot, smelly body.

She needed to answer the call of nature. Grandma had told her to let her know when she felt the need. She would stand guard. "No one will take our dignity away from us, Baby. We don't be no animals."

But it was hard to be so public about every personal need. She was concerned about her hair too. Sections of the cornrows had come undone.

When Grandma and she returned to their place beside Mary Lou, Grandma said, "Gimme your brush, Jade. I'll fix your hair."

Both of them knew that it was important to have your hair brushed and gelled.

"Grandma, will you fix it in a new style of cornrows?" Jade asked. She knew that she would have to sit still for hours getting her hair styled. It would give them something to do to help pass the time and Grandma and she could talk and talk.

Jade squatted down beside Grandma on the burning cement. When Grandma was busy braiding her hair, Jade asked her about the time when, as an infant, she held Grandma's finger so tightly, Grandma had to prise her tiny fingers off to go get her bottle.

"Yeah, you were one month old! When you grabbed my finger and wouldn't let go I knew you were mine," Grandma laughed.

"What about my Mama?" Jade asked. "What happened her?"

Grandma's face clouded over. "Your Mama died when you were born . . . that was terrible," lowering her voice, she added, "Your Mama got involved with the wrong crowd. She didn't even know who your father was."

Jade's heart grew heavy. She was lost in her thoughts

for a while before she asked, "Do I look like my Mama, Grandma?"

"I guess, some. My Keisha was a beautiful-lookin' young girl. You look some like her. Not to say you're not pretty, Jade. I s'pose you look more like me."

Then Grandma said, "Come here," and, wrapping her arms around Jade in a big bear hug, she whispered, "I loved you from the first moment I saw you, Jade."

Jade felt warm and loved. "I love you too, Grandma," she said, giving her grandmother a kiss on the cheek.

Grandma began to rub oil into Jade's scalp as she said tenderly, "Baby, that'll stop the burnin' tinglin' on the top o' your head."

All this time Mary Lou was asleep. When she wakened, Grandma rationed out the bread and water. She had found a bruised orange at the bottom of her bag. The welcome smell of orange wafted over Jade when Grandma was peeling and sectioning it.

When they had finished eating, Grandma took her phone out of her big holdall saying, "Let me see if I can reach Lynn."

She couldn't make a connection.

"Someone said the phone masts have been knocked down by the high winds. But at least we know Lynn and the boys are safe," she said pensively.

Jade wandered off again. She could hear distant noises like the sound of helicopters and dogs barking and yelping. Then she heard a sharp bark quite close. A little black and white Jack Russell with sad brown eyes was tied with a lead to the guardrail on the opposite side to where Grandma, Mary Lou and she had spent the night. Jade had heard dogs barking constantly but never thought that one was so near.

Three tins of unopened food and a painted sign were resting beside the dog. Two small boys, aged about three and four, were sitting on their hunkers looking at the little dog. Jade read aloud from the painted sign, "Will someone take care of my dog, please? Her name is Bunty."

Where is her owner? Jade wondered. *Maybe she was rescued but wasn't allowed to take her dog? She must be heartbroken if she had to leave her pet behind. I wonder if her owner is still alive? She certainly cared about her dog if she left dog food and a sign.*

The two boys watched Jade as she prised open one of the cans. Fortunately, she could get the lid off by pulling back the top with her finger in the small tin loop. She banged the dog food on the ground near the dog and immediately Bunty began to eat it.

"She's hungry like the rest of us," Jade said to the two boys, who were clapping their hands with excitement. Bunty was too busy eating to be bothered by them.

Then in the midst of the darkness of unbelievable misery on the bridge, a spark of light began to shine for Jade. She ran her fingers down the dog's back and stroked the top of her head. When Bunty had finished the can of food, she licked Jade's face with quick, excited, wet touches and wagged her tail furiously. Jade had made a friend at last. She put her head close to the little dog's head and said, "I'll take care of you, Bunty. I've always wanted a dog."

She had wanted a dog for her tenth birthday but Grandma wouldn't hear of it. "That's like another baby in the house. I be too old for babies. I know who'd be left to take care of a dog. NO." Grandma hadn't given her a chance to show that she could be responsible for a pet. Now, she had a little dog to look after. She had food for her and she could walk her with her leash, up and down the bridge.

The little boys petted Bunty until Jade said goodbye, promising to let them see the dog again. As she walked back to Grandma and Mary Lou, pet lovers struck up conversations with her. They wanted to share sad stories. Horror stories of dogs that were terrified by the high winds and ran off never to be seen again. Others were frightened by the rising water and thought they could swim to safety only to give up and drown in front of their owners. Still others were so loved by their owners that the owners refused to leave them behind when they were given the chance to evacuate.

Only God knows what happened to those owners and their pets, Jade thought.

Jade knew that she had to convince Grandma that she could look after Bunty so she walked her back to the opposite guardrail.

"Grandma, I've got a new dog," she announced enthusiastically and before Grandma could say anything, she continued, "Bunty's a gift from God."

Grandma was caught off guard. Her mouth looked tight before she said, "Don't get too attached to that dog, Jade. You'll be broken hearted when you have to leave her behind."

"I won't leave her behind, Grandma. I have food for her and now she's mine," Jade said with conviction.

Grandma left it at that. Jade felt great!

* * *

The time passed much faster with Bunty. It seemed to be a much shorter time the third day, Thursday, before the sun began going down, casting long shadows on the bridge.

The sound of a boat's engine caused the people to surge to the side of the overpass where Mary Lou and Grandma were sitting. Grandma jumped up to make sure that no one trampled on her old neighbour.

A burly man called out from the boat, asking if there was any elderly person there who needed help. Pointing to Mary Lou, Grandma told him that she was old and weak.

"Wherever she goes, my granddaughter and I go too," she said emphatically.

Then a miracle happened! In the midst of all that chaos, when desperate people were clambering to escape from their misery, two young men said, "Stand back. This old woman needs help. We'll carry her to the boat."

They made a chair by holding their hands together and bending low so that Mary Lou could sit on their hands and put her bony arms around their necks. Carefully, they stepped into the boat with her, gently sat her down and, to Jade's amazement, got out again.

Jade had picked up Bunty and her last tin of food. She waited for Grandma to object but she never said a word. Nor did the boatman say anything. Jade's heart was beating excitedly as she climbed into the boat with her little dog under her arm. She found a seat near the boatman.

"That's a nice dog you have," he said, as Jade held Bunty on her knee and rubbed her face in the short hairs on Bunty's back.

"How old is she?" the stranger asked.

Jade's heart stopped and her brain froze over with fear. Grandma, who had sat down beside Mary Lou, said confidently, "Two."

"She's young yet. She can put up with more than us," their rescuer said with a smile.

Jade's nerves were jumping out of her mouth. *Might he find out that Bunty isn't really mine?* she thought fretfully.

"Thank God we're leavin' that bridge," Mary Lou whined. "I won't last much longer. My bones are so sore."

"My back's very sore, too," Grandma said with a pained face, as she stretched her back and then eased it again.

That's the first time since the hurricane that Grandma has complained, Jade thought, as the boat's engine roared into life and they pulled away from the bridge.

XII
Terrible Things

"Hi, folks. I'm John."

"Hi, John. Thanks for comin' to our rescue."

Grandma didn't say anything more after those few words. Jade noticed how exhausted she looked.

"You could do with a drink. You'll find a bottle of water in that sack," Mr John nodded towards a bag lying in the middle of the boat. "There's a couple o' bananas there, too. Potassium. Good for you. My wife insisted on leaving them with me."

Jade reached into the grey sack and took out a two-litre bottle of water and three squishy bananas. She gave the water to Grandma, who took a long drink and held the bottle for Mary Lou to get a drink.

Then Jade took a long drink, before pouring a little

water into her hand for Bunty. The little dog was thirsty too.

Grandma and Mary Lou took their time eating their bananas but Jade peeled back the skin and gobbled hers in three mouthfuls. The little bit at the end she saved for the dog.

For the first time, Jade really looked at the white man who had just rescued them. His strawberry-blond hair was soaking wet and his bleary red eyes were framed by dark circles.

As if to explain his tired looks, he said, "I've only snatched a couple of hours sleep in the past forty-eight hours. I've made a number of rescues with this boat. Oh, God!"

It all seemed to be too much for him and he moved away from them and back into the world of terrible memories for a minute or two. Then, like everyone else, he had to tell what he had experienced.

"I sent my wife and children to Lake Charles on Saturday when the hurricane began to look threatening. I didn't want to take any chances," he paused as if to process what he had just said.

"My wife has kin in Lake Charles. I stayed behind in our house in Bywater. I like the comfort of my own home." He added wryly, "Not that any of us have any comfort now."

Mr John was steering the boat between a row of two-storey houses as he spoke. Jade couldn't recognise where they were. Everywhere had changed so much.

As the boat turned a corner, three people on a veranda screamed for help. Their panic made Jade feel so bad because she could see there was no room left in the small boat that had rescued Grandma, Mary Lou, Bunty and herself.

"God, I can't take another person in this boat. I've seen people jump into a rescue boat and capsize it. A baby drowned. We need the Federal Government's help."

Jade could see that Mr John was stressed out.

"Did y'all know that a twenty-foot tidal surge broke through some levees – you know, the artificial protections built around the banks of the canals, the lake and the river? I saw the water coming up on my porch and then it came into the den. That was about 9 a.m. on Monday," Mr John was standing in the boat paddling through trash as he was talking.

"When I heard the screams for help from people trapped in attics and on rooftops, I took out my fishing boat. It's now Thursday evening and I've been going non-stop. Just snatched a few hours sleep these past few days."

"We were out on the roof too," Mary Lou said in a voice barely beyond a whisper.

Mr John looked at her with dead eyes rimmed in red. Perspiration was running down the sides of his face, down his neck and into his already wet T-shirt which hung limply over his damp denim shorts. He pushed his wet hair out of his eyes and said, "I've seen some terrible things. A middle-aged man and his wife stood in neck-deep water for thirty hours before I rescued them. They couldn't speak. Their eyes were glassy and expressionless. I put them down on a bridge. I hope and pray they got some help."

Mr John continued, "But the worst was when I tried to rescue a family. I was headin' between rows of houses when a young girl's screamin' got my attention. She was hangin' on to a gutter in the water. She told me that she was the only one who could swim. She left her aunt and three cousins in the attic of her aunt's house. When the floodwater kept risin', she jumped into the water and made it through the front door, forced open by the rush of the water," Mr John paused to run the back of his hand along his forehead.

"I had to break through the roof. I was able to rescue her aunt, but her three cousins had panicked 'n' jumped into the water. Their bodies were floatin' in the kitchen. They drowned before they reached the door. God have mercy on them."

Mr John choked up as he said, "One of the girls was about the same age as my eldest daughter. Another looked the same age as you." He nodded towards Jade.

Suddenly, a wave of nausea swept over Jade, "I feel sick, Grandma."

Grandma poured a little water out of the bottle onto a cloth she found in the boat and firstly put the wet rag on her granddaughter's forehead and then on the top of her head.

Jade didn't want to hear any more. *When will all of this pain and agony stop? Will I die? Is this the end of the world? Hell on earth?*

Putting Bunty on the ground, she put her head down on her knees, clapping her hands over her ears. A thought came to her, *Maybe if I keep my eyes and ears closed, this nightmare will go away and life will go back to normal.*

A tiny yelp caught Jade's attention. The little Jack Russell was looking up into her face, her head cocked on one side and sorrow in her brown eyes. It was as if she knew the heartbreak that Jade was experiencing. Jade picked her up, held her close and buried her head in her back. Bunty began to give Jade's face quick wet licks. She made Jade smile again.

Their journey was over when the boat arrived at dry ground outside the New Orleans Ernest N. Morial Convention Center.

"I hope you'll get some help here," Mr John said as he jumped out and pulled the boat up out of the water. He gave a helping hand to each of them.

Mary Lou, Jade and Grandma thanked the Good Samaritan before he jumped back on board.

"That's one good man! He saved our lives," Grandma said as the boat left their sight.

XIII
Waiting

Hundreds of people were wandering around or sitting staring into space outside the Convention Center. They looked like the people on the bridge – dirty, disconnected and desperate.

When Jade had got into the boat from the bridge, she had been sure that at last they were being taken to safety. She couldn't wait to shower and eat decent food.

"Grandma, we should go inside for shelter," Jade said as she took Grandma's and Mary Lou's arms, steering them through the main door of the huge building into the foyer.

A very distressed woman, carrying a small infant, shouted at them as she passed them on her way out, "You don't wanna go in there. It's dark. Hot. Stinkin' like a sewer. Some people are gettin' outta hand."

"She's right," Grandma said. "It's bad enough here. Ugh! Stinkin'. We're better off outside."

Jade could feel her stomach heaving. She held more tightly onto Grandma and Mary Lou's arms, steering them through the crowds and out into the open again.

"Bernice. You shoulda left me in the attic to die. No one cares about us," Mary Lou whimpered.

That's all it took to get Grandma going in a purposeful way again. She spoke firmly, "Don't talk like that, Miss Mary Lou. As long as God gives us life, we'll do the best we can with it. Remember, we're in this together."

Jade could feel Mary Lou leaning even heavier on her arm. The old woman was getting weaker. She needed help. Soon.

A cloud of desperation had settled over the hundreds of hungry, homeless people outside the Convention Center. Many of them had all of their possessions in plastic bags. They had been promised that buses would take them to safety.

They waited.

The buses never came.

Jade noticed a young girl about the same age as herself, holding on one arm a baby of a few months wearing only a diaper, as she wiped the tears off her frightened face with the other hand. "We're gonna die," she sobbed. "People are sayin' they're killin' people in the Superdome. What are we gonna do?"

Jade had no answer for her.

She was struggling to understand what the young girl had just said about the Superdome when suddenly a woman about the same age as Grandma, her hair tidied into small cornrows, the perspiration on her dark face running freely to join her tears, ran out into the middle of the road and knelt down. She joined her hands in supplication and screamed in a loud wail, "Heeeeelp us, pleeeeeeease."

When adults don't have any answers! When they cry in public, what will happen to me? Jade's heart froze over. She began to breathe in short swift gulps. She went back to Grandma.

Seeing her nervousness, Grandma pulled her close, "Baby, stay by me. Everything's gonna be alright. We must keep the faith."

As if responding from the heavens, a Black Hawk helicopter touched down a hundred yards from them. People surged towards it. They were desperate for food and drink.

Grandma did not allow Jade to go over because she was afraid that her granddaughter would be crushed by the angry crowd or hurt by flying bottles.

A young boy, bare to the waist, his body shining with sweat, stopped running long enough to hand Mary Lou a bottle of water. She had curled up on the ground near Grandma.

"Thanks, son," Grandma spoke for Mary Lou, opened the bottle and raised it to her old neighbour's parched mouth. It provided immediate relief.

Jade took some of the water for herself and Bunty.

Jade, Grandma and Mary Lou slept with hundreds of other homeless people on the ground outside the Convention Center that Thursday night.

*　　*　　*

Looking back on that time, all that Jade could recall clearly was waiting. Days slowly melted into each other like candles on a hot plate. They waited in squalor and human waste for two more long days – two thousand, eight hundred and eighty minutes of waiting – hungry, parched, homeless, destitute.

Waiting.
　　　Waiting.
　　　　　Waiting.

While Jade took some comfort from her little dog,

her worries for Grandma and Mary Lou grew by the minute.

An old woman died on the pavement outside the Convention Center. The screams and wails of the dead woman's family tore into Jade's heart. Her tears ran down her face for this stranger and her broken-hearted family. *What would I do if Grandma died?* Jade thought, as a wave of utter loneliness washed over her.

No one in that dead woman's family knew what would happen next. *How could they bury their mother? They could have no funeral service.* The family wailed with grief as they placed a bedcover over their mother's dead body and had to leave her outside the Convention Center in the sweltering heat. Jade shuddered at the misery of it all.

She prayed fervently, *God keep my Grandma safe. Please.*

And Miss Mary Lou, she added.

She was convinced that it was up to her to do everything she could to keep Grandma and Mary Lou from dying. That often meant using a charming smile, kind words or pleas for help just to get a bottle of water or a few pieces of bread.

She learned from experience that people were good and bad. Some shared the last food and water they had. Others bullied and cursed the people who tried to help them.

Mary Lou was getting weaker as she lay on the concrete in the blazing sun. It was so hard to find even a little shade. Grandma put a damp cloth on her friend's head. Jade fanned her with a cardboard box she had flattened.

Jade spotted a young man pushing a mattress on a trolley. She had heard on the bridge that people were looting hotels. She felt that God would understand that some people were stealing because they were desperate. Jade needed that mattress for Mary Lou.

Handing Bunty's leash and her makeshift fan to Grandma, Jade ran over to ask the young man to give up the mattress. Pointing to the still form of Mary Lou, lying on the burning concrete, she pleaded with him, "My old neighbour will die if she doesn't get some help soon."

The young man paused, looked over at Mary Lou, thought about it and then said, "Take it. She's in a bad way."

Jade and Grandma gently lifted Mary Lou onto the thick fresh mattress. Its softness and coolness were a welcome contrast to the heat and hardness of the ground. The old, frail woman muttered her thanks through dry, broken lips.

When Jade and Grandma had made Mary Lou as comfortable as possible, they sat one at each side of the mattress, like sentinels on duty. After some time they fell asleep, propped against a low wall, in the squalor and confusion outside the Convention Center.

XIV
Helicopter Ride

Soldiers with rifles. That's what Jade saw when she opened her eyes on Sunday morning. The National Guard and soldiers from the United States Army were milling around the desperate people outside the Convention Center. She saw them training their guns on people. *Some people musta gone berserk*, Jade thought.

Grandma was awake but Jade wasn't sure about Mary Lou. She was lying with her mouth wide open and her sunken eyes were closed. She didn't seem to be breathing.

"Is Mary Lou alive?" Jade mouthed over to Grandma, who nodded yes.

"I'm goin' over to those soldiers. Miss Mary Lou needs help. You pray, Grandma," Jade said as she got up from the ground and began to walk towards a young soldier with an open friendly face.

* * *

Shortly after that, Grandma began to tell the two soldiers, who came back with Jade to offer to take Mary Lou to a rescue helicopter, that wherever Miss Mary Lou went, she and her granddaughter would also go. She laughed as she described tying the three of them together with an electric cord as they waited on the roof to be rescued.

Jade didn't want to be reminded about that particular ordeal. However, she was now grateful that Grandma had tied them together and had insisted that wherever one went all three would go, especially when she heard from broken-hearted people who had been separated from their family.

Roaming around with Bunty among the despairing people outside the Convention Center, Jade had heard parents wail for children who had been airlifted somewhere . . . but where?

When she told Grandma about the lost children, she said, "That's terrible, Baby. Didn't I tell you? No one will separate us! Don't you see now? It woulda been wrong not to have brought Miss Mary Lou with us?"

Jade thought that Grandma needn't have said the last bit. So much had happened since she had gone next door for Miss Mary Lou. But even though Grandma's comment annoyed her, she didn't suck her lips as she would have done before the storm.

One of the soldiers helping Mary Lou told Grandma that the three of them would be airlifted with a number of other evacuees to Houston, Texas. They would call at Louis Armstrong International Airport, outside New Orleans, first.

"Where is Houston?" Jade asked the soldier with the kind sympathetic face that she had spoken to first.

"It's about three hundred and fifty miles west of New Orleans – in Texas."

"Cool! This will be my first ride in a helicopter."

"You'll ride in a helicopter as far as the airport just outside the city. It's a plane from there to Houston."

"WOW," Jade said with amazement.

"Will Miss Mary Lou get medical help there? What with her age 'n' all," Grandma asked a tall young soldier.

"Yeah. You'll be going to the Astrodome. The Red Cross has set up an emergency medical centre there," he said with a big smile.

"Thank God," Grandma said. Her relief was obvious.

Jade hugged Bunty tightly and rubbed her face through the short hairs on the dog's neck. Bunty belonged to her. They would be going in a helicopter and then in a plane. Jade could hardly contain her excitement: *WHEEEEE . . . YEAH . . . COOOOOOL . . .*

The two young fresh-faced soldiers gently lifted Mary Lou onto a stretcher.

Jade was still holding Bunty in her arms when a soldier with three stripes on his uniform sleeve came up to them. Her heart froze over and stopped when she looked at his stern face. Instinctively, she tightened her arm around Bunty's warm body. Jade's heart began to pound. She held the small dog close. If she had to give up Bunty now, her heart would break into a million bits.

She had heard Grandma say that old Mr Davies had died of a broken heart, shortly after he had found his wife, Bertha, dead in bed beside him. *If Bunty is taken from me now, I know I'll die of a broken heart.*

The soldier hesitated for a moment and then said, "Make sure to keep your arms around that dog and don't let her wander freely. Some of these passengers are old and ill."

Tears trickled down Jade's face. She had heard before that people often cry with relief. Before this, any time she had cried was because she had been angry or hurting in some way. She was now crying happy tears.

She buried her tear-stained face in Bunty's back and her sobs shook her body.

"Baby, have a good cry. You been through so much for a child. I'm glad Bunty's yours," Grandma smiled as she put her arm around her granddaughter.

The noise was deafening as the soldier with the three stripes led Grandma and Jade up to the helicopter steps. The wind created by the revolving rotary blades nearly blew Jade off her feet. Grandma helped her keep her balance because she had her knapsack on her back and she was carrying Bunty and Mary Lou's big black bag.

Jade was very excited when she got inside the helicopter. She stared around her at the big grey shell with no seats. She hadn't imagined a helicopter to be like this. *Come to think of it, I've never ever thought about the inside of a helicopter.*

Mary Lou and two other elderly people were on stretchers at the back. There was room near Mary Lou so Grandma and Jade sat there on the floor.

"We're just beside you, Miss Mary Lou," Grandma whispered into her old friend's ear.

Jade thought she could see a little smile struggling around Mary Lou's pale, dry lips but she didn't open her eyes.

"Thank God we on our way," Grandma whispered to Jade, who could hardly wait for the helicopter to lift off.

The stern-faced soldier came up to them and said, "The airport in New Orleans has been turned into a hospital. Other sick and injured people will join you for the journey to Houston. You'll be continuing your journey in a medical plane." He then sat down near the pilot of the helicopter.

"How can an airport be turned into a hospital?" Jade asked Grandma, picturing, on one hand, the long wards smelling of disinfectant that she walked through when Grandpa was ill and, on the other, Louis Armstrong International Airport milling with excited travellers when Uncle Jordan flew home from boot camp.

"Can't imagine it," Grandma replied solemnly.

"Anyway we're on our way, Grandma," Jade said as she felt the helicopter lift off the ground.

She began to feel excited again. Flying in a helicopter now, and then in a plane to Houston. She had never left Louisiana before.

XV
Hell and Heaven

The helicopter glided down on the tarmac near the main terminal. It had been a very short journey from the Convention Center to Louis Armstrong International Airport on the outskirts of New Orleans.

When the door opened, Jade could see a large grey plane with a huge opening in the back. People were being carried into it from baggage trolleys that were transporting the sick and elderly.

The soldier with three stripes on his sleeve arrived back with a young, tousled-haired man wearing large brown-framed glasses and a worried expression. "This is Dr Trimble," the soldier said. "He'll examine all of the stretcher people."

The doctor took Mary Lou's pulse and sounded her heart. "We'll make you good for the journey. We'll give you some fluids. Drink plenty of water," Dr Trimble said as he moved on to examine the other people on stretchers.

The soldier in charge handed Grandma a six-pack of bottled water and ordered two young soldiers to begin carrying the stretchers into the large military plane.

They picked up Mary Lou. Grandma and Jade followed the stretcher. This time, Jade hardly noticed the noise and the wind created by the helicopter's big rotary blades. Her attention was drawn to a Continental Airlines baggage trolley being driven towards the plane. She could see an old person strapped to a stretcher, a middle-aged man sitting on the side, his head wrapped in bandages, and a young girl, about her own age, who was holding an IV bag, which was attached to her arm. The baggage trolley stopped as two young women went over to help the patients transfer to the plane.

Jade began to think about travelling in the plane. She had always wanted to fly. In many of her dreams she was flying high above the clouds. Now she had mixed emotions. This plane was like a flying ambulance. She would be travelling with injured and sick people. *It sure won't be a fun trip*, she thought.

A ramp had been lowered at the back of the plane. Jade couldn't really see the inside until she reached the top of the ramp. She thought it looked like a gigantic grey cave. It was a big empty shell with all kinds of gadgetry, screens and wires along the high walls. *Even the soldiers look small inside this plane.* Stretchers were lined on the floor to the back of the plane. Jade noticed the people from the Continental baggage vehicle.

Mary Lou was lying on the end of the second row of three rows of stretchers. Jade and Grandma picked their steps to sit on the floor on each side of her.

Soon the big door at the back of the plane banged closed and the interior lights came on automatically. The man with the bandaged head came up to sit on a bench near Jade and Grandma. He told everyone in his hearing that the airport had been converted into a hospital. Patients were lying on the baggage carousels. Many were screaming with pain and there wasn't enough medication to go around. He had heard on a short-wave radio that a Chinook helicopter had come under fire from snipers when it tried to evacuate patients from a hospital.

"See that Chinook! It's good for speedy lift off and set down. I flew in one of them when I served with the US Air Force in Vietnam. I was a sergeant."

"How many stripes does a sergeant have?" Jade asked.

"Three," answered the former soldier.

Jade made a mental note that the serious soldier with three stripes on his sleeve was a sergeant.

Just then a loudspeaker system crackled into operation and the serious sergeant announced, "Welcome on board the United States Air Force C-17 Globemaster III. This plane has been used in Iraq and Afghanistan to transport troops and armoured vehicles. Now it's being used as a military ambulance. We'll land at Houston Airport in one hour and twenty-three minutes. Enjoy the flight."

Jade noticed a young girl with a very pale face, framed with damp blonde hair, lying with closed eyes next to Mary Lou. A woman, who looked like her mother, sat on the floor behind her, fanning the young girl's face with a piece of cardboard. She looked haggard and dishevelled, her wet brown hair tied back off her weather-beaten, long, thin face with an old scarf. Her eyes had a vacant dark stare. They looked as if they had gone back into her head because they had seen too much.

Jade wondered if her own eyes had gone away back into her head. She had seen so many terrible things.

Grandma spoke in a very sympathetic voice to the sad woman, "Is that your little girl, Ma'am?"

Barely above a whisper, the woman answered, "Yeah – this is my youngest – Summer. She went into herself when my husband died. She refused to eat or talk. God, I don't need to lose her too."

She stopped to draw her breath then continued, "He had a bad heart and he died just as we were being rescued from the attic." Dropping her voice to a tiny whisper, almost as if she could hardly form the words for herself or anyone else, she said, "We were three days in the attic. We had just drunk our last bottle of water when we were taken out by boat. Summer took it hard when her daddy died."

The woman spoke in a monotone as if all the emotion in her body had been wrung out like a wet cloth in a mangle. The words came low and slow like the last drips of water.

"If only help had come even one day sooner."

"I'm sorry, Ma'am," Grandma whispered. Her eyes were full of tears and the sides of her mouth quivered.

Jade noticed and felt terrible. She looked at the little girl who was about six or seven years old. She felt so sorry for her. Summer would never see her father again. Jade knew that it was different for her. She had never known her father. *I would have liked to know my daddy. But I don't.*

With Bunty under her arm, Jade crawled along the floor until she was just beside the little girl. She put her pet down between Summer and Miss Mary Lou.

"Bunty, you must be Summer's friend too," she whispered into Bunty's ear.

Calling the little girl in a quiet coaxing voice she said, "Summer, I've got a little dog here. Would you like to see her?"

The little girl opened her soft blue eyes. It seemed to take ages for her to focus. When she did catch sight of Bunty, she smiled and slowly took her hand out from under the green army blanket. She ran her fingers gently along the dog's back and stroked her between her ears. Bunty moved closer, wagging her tail. It was almost as if she knew how traumatised the little blonde-haired girl was and how much she needed her. Summer kept running her hand down Bunty's back and petting her head. Jade decided to leave Bunty with her for a while. She felt so sad for the little girl.

Everywhere they went, things were chaotic and everyone had hair-raising stories to tell. Jade wondered if life now was going to be one terrible thing after another. *Hell is eternal suffering. We have fallen into hell*, she thought again.

The bigger girl with the IV in her arm was silent and withdrawn. The man with the bandaged head said that she was his daughter. His wife and other children had been taken to Houston when he and his daughter were brought for medical help to the airport.

The stern sergeant came up to Jade. She got so nervous when he came towards her that her mouth suddenly became dry and her tongue felt like a big stone that she couldn't move. Now she knew what people meant when they said someone was tongue-tied. She was tongue-tied now. Her heart skipped a beat. She was afraid of what the soldier was going to say.

Without a smile, he stood as if to attention and said, "Miss, I want you to take your dog and hold him until we land in Houston."

Jade felt her body go limp with relief. "Okay," she managed to say, before crawling quickly over to Summer to tell her what the sergeant had said. The little girl gave a wan smile and nodded.

"Thanks, love," Summer's mother said to Jade.

Jade picked up Bunty and held her close to her face saying, "You're a great little dog and you're mine."

She shuffled back to be near Grandma and lay down beside her with her arm around Bunty. On falling asleep, she dreamed that she had wings on her back and was flying to a beautiful island of palm trees and bleached white sandy beaches. As soon as she landed there, a little Jack Russell ran up to her from behind one of the palm trees. Bunty stood on her back legs and put her front paws into her hands while wagging her tail furiously. Then she lay down, rolled over on her back with her paws in the air and Jade rubbed her tummy. When she jumped up excitedly, they both ran along the beach until they caught up with Grandma and Mary Lou, who were strolling along, talking and laughing, without a care in the world.

"This is heaven" Grandma said when Jade joined them.

"It sure is," Mary Lou said, "How will I ever be able to repay the both of you for your kindness to me?"

"I'm glad you're with us in heaven. I thought we were goin' to be in hell for ever and ever," Jade said with a laugh.

A sudden bump and rasping sound wakened Jade from her sleep. They were still in the plane. They must have landed in Houston.

XVI
Houston

"We've arrived at our destination. Wheelchairs will be waiting for those who need them. A bus will bring you to the Astrodome, an emergency site for evacuees. The Red Cross will take care of your needs. It has been a pleasure travelling with you." The serious sergeant turned off the microphone just before the large, garage-like, back door slid up.

Jade could see the terminal buildings of Houston Airport. A group of men and women wearing white vests with large red crosses on their backs and name tags with red crosses on their chests, were waiting to enter the plane. Some of them were pushing wheelchairs. One of them came up the ramp first and asked everyone who could walk to leave the plane and stand to the left.

"We'll wait for you on the tarmac outside the plane, Miss Mary Lou," Grandma reassured her old friend.

"Mind my bag," Mary Lou whispered to Jade, who was clutching Bunty under one arm and carrying Mary Lou's big black bag on the other.

Jade looked around for Summer but she was nowhere to be seen. She was sorry that she hadn't really said a proper goodbye to her.

"Wait a minute, Baby. Let me help you put your knapsack on your back," Grandma said as she lifted Jade's knapsack off the floor.

Jade quickly set down the big black bag and Bunty, putting each arm into the straps of the knapsack being held out by Grandma. Her bag was a lot lighter now because they had thrown away some of her dirty clothes. There had been nowhere to wash anything since they climbed into the attic and out to the roof. *Hope my charm bracelet's safe*, Jade thought, a jab of fear in her chest. She swung her knapsack off again to unzip the front pocket. The little blue box was there.

"Now you feel better, Baby," Grandma said gently as she held out the straps again.

With the knapsack on her back, Jade picked up Bunty, holding her under her arm. Carrying Mary Lou's bag on her other arm, she began to walk down the ramp into the bright sunshine. Red Cross people greeted them with smiles as three luxury coaches drew up alongside the plane.

"Hi, everyone. Welcome to Houston. We want to get you out of this heat as soon as possible. When your sick family members are seated you can make your way to them," a Red Cross man with a round, kind face, red cheeks and grey eyes under black bushy eyebrows told the bedraggled group of evacuees.

Bunty was wriggling to get down. Jade knew that the little Jack Russell needed some exercise having been cooped up for so long. Turning towards the kind Red Cross man whose name tag said 'Tim', Jade asked, "Mr Tim, is it alright to give my dog a little run?"

"Sure. That's a nice dog you have."

Grandma took Mary Lou's bag and Jade set off at a trot with her little dog running in front of her. For the first time in nearly a week she was running free.

*   *   *

Grandma and Jade boarded the coach and went to sit near Mary Lou. Although Grandma's old friend was weak, she was breathing better in the cool air of the coach.

Suddenly, Mary Lou became agitated and asked, "Have you got my bag, Jade?"

"Yeah, here it is," Jade said, holding out the bag. She knew that Mary Lou didn't want to be parted from her big black bag for any length of time so she put it on the old woman's lap. Mary Lou smiled with relief and gratitude.

The air conditioning was much colder than it had been in the large military plane. Grandma told Jade that she could sit near a window for the twenty-three mile journey south to the Astrodome. Jade put Bunty on the seat beside her, where she curled up and went to sleep. But the little dog soon woke up when she began to sniff a special smell from life before the storm.

Jade's mouth started to water as she began to picture a giant burger, so big that she had to break off pieces for Grandma, Mary Lou and, of course, Bunty. She found it hard to control herself and stay in her seat as Mr Tim began passing out hamburgers and French fries in the familiar Burger King bags. "My favourite food!" Jade excitedly told Grandma.

"Yeah. Thank God for small mercies," Grandma said as she stood up to put her big holdall onto the overhead rack so as to free some space on her lap for the food.

Afterwards, when Jade was biting into her hamburger, eating her fries and drinking cola, she thought all her birthdays had come together.

Bunty wolfed down the bits of hamburger meat Jade broke off for her. When everything was finished, she sat with her ears up and her eyes focused on Jade's hands.

"No more, Bunty. All gone."

When the dog was really sure that there was no more food, she eased down on the seat and curled up again for a sleep.

The sun shone brightly in a clear blue sky as the coach pulled out of the airport. Jade felt better than she had felt for days. She was amazed that everything looked so normal. Cars and trucks were speeding along regular highways. Trees shaded tidy gardens.

But it was the brightly coloured shops with their displays of clothes, televisions, furniture and food that built up her excitement. People were talking and laughing as they sat outside restaurants, shaded from the hot sun by colourful umbrellas. Her heart raced. *They look soooo cool. Soooo normal.*

It all reminded her of how New Orleans was before the storm, when Grandma would drive her and Natasha in her old Chevy to the mall. *Where is Natasha now?*

Her thoughts went to the time in St Albert's when they had a special performance of the school band, cheerleaders and majorettes in the gym hall. *Everyone was so excited and happy. Me, Natasha and some friends ate pizza afterwards . . . Mr Cooper came over to tell us how well we'd performed . . . I wonder what happened to him . . . and David?* Jade's mood darkened when she recalled that she had been dressed in her worst gear when she had last seen David in Walmart before the storm. *Surely he evacuated when the water came up*, she thought.

*   *   *

"We've reached the Astrodome," announced the Red Cross man who had travelled with them from the airport in Houston. "Please don't move until you have been given directions."

Jade sat with her face pressed against the glass, transfixed by the sight in front of her. Thousands of stressed-looking people were milling around the Astrodome. Her heart sank down, down, down. She wondered if she was going to be an evacuee for the rest of her life.

The coach door opened and two Red Cross volunteers boarded. They came up to Mary Lou, gently helping her to her feet and half-carrying her to the back and down a ramp to a waiting wheelchair.

"My bag, Jade," she called over her shoulder.

"Okay, Miss Mary Lou. Don't worry, I'm holding it for you," Jade told her.

With a heavy heart, Jade put her knapsack on her back, picked up Mary Lou's bag with one hand and scooped Bunty up and under her arm with the other.

A Red Cross lady with frizzy blonde hair and tiny glasses on the end of her nose directed Grandma and Jade down the ramp to join Mary Lou. The lady's name tag read 'Sophie'.

"Let me push you, Miss Mary Lou," Jade offered when she joined Mary Lou. Putting the big black bag on her old neighbour's knees, she gently took the handles of the wheelchair, turning it round towards the huge building that had been pointed out to them as the Astrodome.

"You need to register in the lobby," Sophie called out after Jade. A lot of people were crowding the Red Cross volunteers, asking questions and showing their nervousness.

"Take your time, Baby," Grandma said as she double-checked the number of bags that she had taken off the coach.

It was a blistering hot day but they didn't have far to push the wheelchair before they went through a double glass door into another world. Jade's heart began to pound. Grandma and Mary Lou were silent. They were in the foyer of the Astrodome in Houston, Texas.

XVII

The Astrodome

"Oh God. Grandma, look at this!" Jade's eyes were wide open at the scene in front of her.

She was standing with Bunty under her arm, holding on to Mary Lou's wheelchair. They had arrived at the door to the main arena of the Houston Astrodome, which had been converted from an indoor stadium into an emergency evacuation centre. Grandma, Mary Lou and Jade were joining the thousands of men, women and children – storm debris of New Orleans – who had been evacuated there.

People were sitting or lying on small narrow beds, military cots, row after tightly packed row, stretching out as far as Jade could see. The cots reminded her of the blue metal-framed bed that she had lain on to take a nap when she was in kindergarten.

Many people were walking around between the narrow beds. Jade thought that the most shocking thing about this scene was that all of these people were like herself: homeless. She realised that this football stadium was going to be her home indefinitely. A tear slid down her face.

"Grandma, I'll never be able to get used to bein' around so many people. Remember, it was just me and you in New Orleans."

"Yeah, Baby, it's hard. I heard someone say that there are fifteen thousand people here. Fifteen thousand people with no home to go to! . . . But one good thing. We're safe . . . thank God."

Many people were wandering around with the same dazed look that Jade had seen on the faces of the people on the bridge and outside the Convention Center.

She overheard a man asking if anyone had seen his ten-year-old daughter. He carried a big piece of cardboard with the words '*Tyler, call Daddy at 504-281-7763*'.

One woman told Grandma she wanted to find her brother, who had phoned her from a rooftop as he waited to be rescued. "Maybe I'll find him here," she said hopefully as she shuffled towards the main hall.

"Little girl, you need to bring that dog over here," ordered a balding man, wearing khaki pants, white shirt and a Red Cross vest. He pointed to Bunty as he spoke.

Jade tightened her hold on her little dog. The Red Cross man smiled as he said, "It's alright. We've a place for pets on the side of the arena. We've food and space for them where they can run and play. It's a rule not to have dogs where you have so many people indoors."

On seeing Jade's crestfallen face, the Red Cross man said kindly, "You can visit your pet every day. There'll be a set time. You'll be able to arrange the time with the ASPCA. I'll get you a pass."

Jade's heart was beating furiously and her tongue was sticking to the roof of her mouth. She was breathing in shallow, quick bursts. *He'll see my nervousness and know Bunty isn't mine. Then he'll take her off me.* She took a big breath and told herself, *But Bunty is mine now.* These words steadied her.

Lifting up the little dog's name tag, the man said, "I see her name's Bunty and there's a phone number on her collar."

The man thought for a minute and then said, "Oh, but of course, this phone number'll be no good since the storm."

The man couldn't know that this phone number belonged to someone else, Jade told herself fearfully. She didn't need to tell him that this little Jack Russell was her hurricane pet, even though she felt a little guilty and even deceitful.

"Jade, it's alright. Bunty'll be safe and you'll be able to see her every day," Grandma put her arm around Jade's shoulder. It gave her strength.

"Here you are!" came the cheerful voice as the Red Cross man handed Jade a pass to see Bunty. Turning to Grandma he said, "Ma'am, when you get your sick friend situated, come round to the right side as you're facing the main entrance going in to the Astrodome. You'll see the fenced off area for the animals. Just present your pass."

While Grandma was thanking him, Jade was struggling with a big lump that had come up in her throat. She looked down at Bunty. The little dog was holding her head to the side. She was looking at Jade with sad, soft brown eyes.

"Don't worry, Bunty. I'll be around to see you as soon as we have seen to Miss Mary Lou. Remember, you're my special little dog," Jade scooped Bunty up and gave her a kiss before she put her down on the ground again and handed her leash to the Red Cross man.

The tears, which were always lurking just behind her lower eyelids, welled up and began to trickle slowly down her cheeks as she watched him walk out the side door with her little dog.

Jade rubbed the tears away with the back of her hand. Grandma needed her to go with her and Mary Lou to the medical area. They pushed the wheelchair to a makeshift screen that had a printed notice, 'DO NOT GO BEYOND THIS POINT', hanging in view. Jade and Grandma stopped.

A smiling nurse said, "Hi. What can I do for you?"

Grandma showed her Mary Lou's water tablets and gave her all her old neighbour's details.

"Will you step outside while the doctor examines your friend, please," the kind nurse with big blue eyes and dimples in her cheeks said. "She looks dehydrated so we'll put her on a drip for a while. Maybe you could go away for about an hour and then check back with us."

"Grandma, can we go and check on Bunty?" Jade whispered as they left the medical centre.

"Not yet, Baby. We must get ourselves situated first."

A woman dressed in a Red Cross vest was directing people to line up to register for special orange wristbands. Jade and Grandma got into line. So many people were walking around nervous and sad that Jade found herself searching faces to see if she could recognise anyone. Finally, Grandma and she reached the table and got a wristband each and one for Mary

Lou. Their names were printed in black on the orange plastic bands.

They're the kind that once they're closed on your wrist they have to be cut off. We had them for the rides in the school fair. I wonder why we need them here? Jade thought.

"Come on Jade. Let's get Miss Mary Lou," Grandma said pulling Jade's arm with the new wristband and heading back into a big crowd. Jade allowed herself to be led by Grandma to the medical centre at the other end of the lobby and through a double door to the familiar sign. They re-joined the line and when it was their turn to see the nurse, Grandma asked for Miss Mary Lou Smith. After about a minute, their old neighbour was wheeled out wearing a new set of clothes, grey pants and a blue turtle-neck top. Her eyes looked brighter and she was smiling.

Jade smelled perfume as she stepped forward to take hold of the handles of the wheelchair, "You look good, Miss Mary Lou. That's a nice smell. What is it?"

"Eau de cologne," the old woman answered and smiled. Gently, Jade pushed her to the side while the nurse was talking to Grandma. She overheard the words 'dehydrated' and 'underweight' before she gently clasped the orange band onto Mary Lou's wrist, saying, "We're evacuees. We all have to wear these, Miss Mary Lou."

Mary Lou turned the band round to read her name and then said, "An evacuee at eighty-nine. Oh, God!" Jade swallowed a lump in her throat. *This is all so hard for an old woman*, she thought.

"Come back again in two days and do make sure that your friend drinks plenty of water in the meantime." The nurse's voice was loud and clear.

Two days! . . . Maybe someone will rescue us before that. Jade began to think how much her life had changed. *Will it ever be like it used to be when I was at school with my friends? . . . We had so much fun . . . Maybe I'll meet some kids here?* Jade's spirits began to lift.

Mary Lou, in a voice a little above a whisper, broke into her reverie, "Jade, I feel a whole lot better now."

"That's great, Miss Mary Lou," Jade said enthusiastically.

"I think we're in the right place," Grandma, who had just joined them, added. "I feel good about that."

Jade looked from Grandma to Mary Lou. Grandma's face seemed a little more relaxed. Though Mary Lou had said that she felt much improved, Jade knew that she still needed a lot of care.

XVIII
Spaghetti with Italian-Style Meat Sauce

"We haven't seen yet where we'll be spendin' the night," Grandma said as she pointed to the main door from the lobby into the huge arena.

A kind-faced woman, wearing a Red Cross name tag, 'SUE', came over to them and said with a warm sympathetic smile, "Ladies, are you looking for somewhere to put your things? Please follow me." She led the way up the arena, through a maze of beds and people, stopping in a corner, near a five-foot wall jutting out from the bleachers.

"Are these alright for you? I thought you might like a little area where you can manage a wheelchair and be able to move around easier."

Jade stared at the small space and the three narrow beds. She was caught in that moment when you hear something and your eyes and mind have to make sense of it.

"Is this it?" she said, her voice betraying confused feelings.

"Thanks, Sue," Mary Lou spoke next. "It'll be nice to have a bed of your own."

"Yeah. Thank God for some comfort and a space that's ours," Grandma said as she began to push Mary Lou's wheelchair closer to the wall jutting out from the bleachers. "I tell ye, it's a million times better than sleepin' on the hard ground."

"What bed'll you take, Baby?" Grandma asked Jade who was just standing there, daydreaming about her bedroom at home with its pretty pink headboard and matching bedspread.

"Which one's yours Grandma?"

"Miss Mary Lou, will this one beside the wall be good for you?" Grandma asked her old neighbour.

"Anywhere at all, Bernice . . . Okay, I suppose that's good."

"Then I'll take the one at the edge," Jade said as she swung her knapsack onto it. *I'd rather Grandma be beside Mary Lou in case there's an emergency*, she thought.

"Jade, will you come to get something to eat for y'all?" Sue asked, touching Jade's elbow.

She led Jade down a path between rows of cots.

"How will I be able to find my way around here?" Jade shouted above the noise of thousands of displaced people asking a million questions of everyone.

"Just remember that your cots are in the left corner at the back as you walk through the main door into the arena. When you're lying on them, you're directly facing the front of the Astrodome. The wall jutting out from the bleachers should make it easier for you," Sue advised.

Jade didn't feel confident about finding their place again. "Baby, you'd get lost in a brown paper bag," Grandma had told her once when she got lost at the mall. She had run ahead to pay for parking as Grandma's legs were tired. She got all turned around then and went in the opposite direction. That was scary.

Now she tried to visualise how to go from the corner at the back of the arena, through the sea of people milling around, out the main door and to the left, not right, to visit Bunty. But that would be later. She was hungry and couldn't wait to eat. It was a good while since she had eaten the burger.

As she was following Sue out a side door into another large room, a thought occurred to Jade and turning towards the kind Red Cross woman, she asked in a pleading voice, "Can we have two mattresses, please? One for Miss Mary Lou and one for my grandmother. They've sore backs from lying on the hard ground."

"But of course, Jade," Sue graciously replied.

She turned back to ask some young men wearing smaller Red Cross badges to help take two mattresses down from a pile near the tables and to bring them into the stadium where the wall juts out near the bleachers on the left side.

"The food's next door, Jade," she said. "I'll show you so that you'll know what to do next time."

* * *

As they stood in line and Jade was answering Sue's questions about her experiences in the hurricane, Jade thought it was strange that there was no smell of food being cooked. Before they reached the top of the line, Sue had explained to her that they would be eating MREs: Meals Ready to Eat.

"They're usually sent to the military. You're gettin' them because there's too many people to cook for in this shelter."

The MREs were stacked in high piles on tables manned by volunteers. Jade noticed that Sue picked up three brown sealed pouches with large black printing on the outside:

MRE SPAGHETTI
with Italian-Style Meat Sauce

She handed them to Jade saying, "Honey, there's an instant heater pad inside . . . Make sure you follow the instructions . . . You know your way back to the corner, don't you? . . . I've to do another job."

Jade was in a kind of trance. So many changes. Now the kind lady was leaving her. In a fog of confusion, she thanked Sue and, clutching the three brown packets, turned back hoping to find her way to their makeshift home in the huge arena.

Did Sue say there was a heater pad inside these? Jade asked herself as she looked at the packets in her hand and could feel nothing rectangular and hard. *I can't imagine how there are heater pads in these*, she thought.

Later, when she was reading the directions to Grandma, who couldn't read without her glasses, she discovered how the heating in the pouch worked. The

Spaghetti and Meat Sauce was already pre-cooked. It would heat up when they would pour salty water into the pouch and leave it for fifteen minutes.

"Chemical reaction. Cool, Grandma!" Jade said. She was delighted also when she discovered an oatmeal cookie, raisins, a spoon, salt and pepper and a towelette in another pouch.

"No ordinary pouch," Grandma said with a laugh.

While they were waiting for their food to heat up, Jade helped Grandma to make up the beds with the new mattresses. She was happy that Grandma and Mary Lou would be sleeping on comfortable beds.

*   *   *

After they had eaten and cleared away their meal, Jade wandered over to the clothes table at the far side of the arena. She was thinking about the MRE. *It was okay*, she told herself. A tall, bright-skinned girl, who resembled Beyoncé Knowles, was at the table with a shorter dark-skinned girl wearing big dangly earrings. The girl like Beyoncé wore a cute pink top with a heart encased in tiny white pearls over tight blue jeans and New Balance tennis shoes. The other girl was laughing loudly as she held a bright red top up against herself. "How do you like the 'Lady in Red'?" she was asking.

"That's a nice colour on you," Jade ventured to say.
The girls seemed to be the same age as herself so she found it easy to talk to them. She soon discovered that the two girls had just met each other minutes before at the table. The tall girl who looked like Beyoncé said that her name was Lirette. She had been evacuated by boat from New Orleans East. The other girl, Brittany, said that she had gone with her family to her aunt's house in Gentilly, near St Albert's School. When the floodwaters began to rise, they sought refuge in the school.

"That's my school," Jade said excitedly.

"Oh, you should see it now," Brittany said, shaking her head slowly from side to side and pursing her lips, hand on hips. "It was horrible . . . The water kept coming up so we went to the second floor . . . We were stranded . . . We had to be rescued by helicopter from the walkway between the two buildings."

Jade's heart sank. She knew exactly where Brittany was talking about. She tried to picture her new classroom but a grey mist covered it. Even her image of Mr Cooper was blurred. She told the girls about escaping to the roof of her house in the Ninth Ward and being tied to her Grandma and an old white neighbour with an electric cord. Although she felt her story was the worst by far, the girls didn't show any real surprise. Everyone lived with horrible memories and had shocking stories to tell.

Realising that she had something cheerful to talk about, Jade told the girls that she had a little dog in the animal enclosure.

"I'd like to check on her," Jade said.

"Gee, you're lucky having your pet with you," Lirette said enthusiastically. "So many people had to leave their pets behind."

Jade felt a bit strange knowing the truth about Bunty. *Should I tell her how I found the little dog tied to a guardrail on a bridge?* Jade asked herself.

"Would you like to come with me to see Bunty?"

"YEAH!" Lirette and Brittany shouted in unison.

XIX
Living in the Astrodome

"Where's that pass?" Jade murmured as she searched in her shorts' pockets for the pass she got when they'd just arrived and she had to give up Bunty.

"I have to show my pass somewhere in order to get into the animal enclosure," Jade said distractedly to Lirette and Brittany. "Ah, here it is," she said as it fell out of a bundle of tissues.

They were happy as they made their way out of the Astrodome by the double doors to the left.

Jade followed the noise of barking and yelping dogs to the enclosure where the pets were being kept. A big sign on the fence read 'ASPCA Shelter'. A young woman wearing a name tag 'MIA', was checking the passes.

Later, Jade tried to figure out if Bunty had come dashing towards her because she saw her or because she had heard her say her name. Whichever it was, all Jade saw at the time was a black and white blur flying towards her at the fence. *It's soooo hard to have a fence separating me from my little pet*, Jade thought.

"Will you keep your eye on Bunty and talk to her while I show my pass?" she asked her new friends.

To Bunty she said, "Good girl, I'm coming."

Jade began to rush in Mia's direction but she found it hard to take her eyes off her little barking pet. As she joined the line of pet owners waiting to get into the enclosure, she shouted over her shoulder, "Tell her I'm comin' now."

Jade kept looking over to where she had left the two girls as she inched closer to the gate and Mia. She saw her new friends kneeling down to pet Bunty. With their fingers poked through the chain-link fence, they were stroking the top of her head.

Jade couldn't wait to rub Bunty's tummy and watch her roll over with her paws in the air, barking with excitement and pleasure.

At last, she was showing her pass to the young girl with long black hair, piercing grey eyes and a freckled face.

"Hi, which dog is yours?" Mia asked.

"The black and white Jack Russell. Bunty," Jade

rushed the words. Urgency and excitement made her speak very fast.

"She's a very friendly dog. Enjoy your visit. You've thirty minutes," Mia said as she handed Jade a leash.

"Can my friends come in too?" Jade asked nodding to the side.

"Sure!"

Jade, Lirette and Brittany bounded through the gate. A little black and white ball hurtled into Jade. She found herself trying to hug a jumping, panting Bunty that licked her face and hands with her warm, wet tongue. Jade couldn't hold her. She leapt and wriggled from her to the ground, racing round and round, wagging her stump of a tail. With the jumps, tail wagging, barking and rolling, paws in the air and "Fiff, Fiff, Fiffing" from Bunty, Jade laughed and laughed.

Free. Warm. Loved. Happy. Very happy.

After a while, the little Jack Russell calmed down. The girls took turns walking her on her leash around the perimeter of the enclosure. After thirty minutes, Mia came over saying, "Sorry. Time's up. You can come back tomorrow and the three of you can walk dogs that need exercise, including Bunty of course. How 'bout that?"

"Sounds good," Jade answered, feeling that Bunty was in safe hands, which made leaving her a bit easier.

Jade and her two friends talked and laughed about dogs until they reached the inside of the arena, where they parted company, saying they would see each other in the lobby at 11 a.m. the next day.

On her way back through the rows and rows of beds, Jade thought how lucky she was to have a little pet in Houston, especially when she saw the people lying on their cots staring vacantly around them or up at the ceiling. Some had pulled the covers over their heads. *They want to be left alone*, Jade thought. *It's sad to think they lost everything.*

Three men in black hats, black suits and with rather large, bushy beards were walking up one aisle, pausing to talk to the people. Some of the men and women who had hidden their heads under their blankets pulled them down to speak to the men but others didn't want to talk and stayed under their blanket retreats. The darkly dressed strangers moved slowly out of sight.

"Did you talk to those men in dark suits, Grandma?" Jade asked when she reached their corner.

"Yeah. Jewish Rabbis, Jade. Good people. They gave me a few dollars to buy a treat for Miss Mary Lou."

Grandma was fingering a fifty dollar bill as she said, "I'm not sure where I'll be able to buy a treat – I was just thinkin' about that." Then she paused for a moment before saying, "You missed the Catholic nuns! You should've seen the excitement of that man over there when he saw them." She nodded over to where a middle-aged man was sitting on the edge of his cot reading the paper. "He got up off his bed and shouted, 'Thank you Jesus. It's alright, our Sisters are here.' To tell you the truth . . . I had to shed a few tears myself . . . After the nuns had gone, he told me they had taught his only daughter, who is now living in Atlanta . . . She called when the hurricane first went into the Gulf askin' them to come to her . . . They felt they were safe . . . Their house had never flooded . . . They had to be rescued off a bridge . . . just like us."

"That's terrible, Grandma. I wonder how Sr Margarita and the other nuns made out in the hurricane?"

"Hope they're safe. That man has faith, Baby. He said, 'God gave and God has taken away. We have been blessed.'"

"How can you say you're blessed if you've lost everything?" Jade said with annoyance.

"Well, they may have lost material things – but they still have their lives, Jade."

Thinking over what Grandma had just said, Jade was quiet for a few minutes. Then she began to talk about Bunty. She told Grandma and Mary Lou that she would be going back to visit Bunty with her new friends, Lirette and Brittany, in the morning.

Grandma said with a warm smile, "Your little dog's a blessin'."

Not too long after that, when she was lying in her cot, Jade smiled thinking about Bunty. She was so happy that Grandma hadn't objected to the little dog. Jade knew that Grandma always wanted the best for her. Didn't she work hard to send her to a fee-paying school? It was so sad to think that Grandma had lost everything in the storm. It would be very tough for her to start over. And their old neighbour. *How could Mary Lou start all over again?* Jade told herself she'd help them both.

It wasn't long before she fell asleep.

XX

Meeting Summer Again

"Let's see what's happenin' in the outside world," Grandma said with enthusiasm, grabbing a handle of Mary Lou's wheelchair and pushing it sharply towards the lobby.

They had just finished breakfast and Grandma wanted to see some TV. The lobby, was full of people. Lost. Distracted. Nervous. Fill-in-the-time people. Over in one corner a TV blared the news. A small group had pulled chairs over to the television and were sitting in a cluster around it.

Jade's attention was caught by something else. A line of people curling towards two tables where she could see telephones. People had been saying that all communication by phone had been destroyed by the high winds. Now she could see eight phones on two tables. *Great! I'll be able to call Natasha*, she thought.

Standing for a few minutes at the television, Jade heard that 80 per cent of the city of New Orleans had been flooded. Their area, the Ninth Ward, was one of the worst. The television announcer said that some houses there had split in half. She shuddered at the memory of the house she saw breaking in two. The falling woman's screams chilled her heart. Jade suddenly felt very cold.

"What about our house?" she asked Grandma when she felt she could speak again.

Grandma looked worried and old when Jade looked into her face. "Dunno, Baby," she whispered, a faraway look in her eyes.

Jade wanted to break out of the pain of memories and the emptiness, "Grandma, I'm gonna join that phone line."

Grandma nodded, but Jade knew that her mind was in one place.

NEW ORLEANS
The Home of JAZZ
THE BIG EASY
The City that Care forgot
Party City USA

DESTROYED. DEVASTATED. DROWNED.
DESTROYED. DEVASTATED. DROWNED.
DESTROYED. DEVASTATED. DROW . . .

*   *   *

Armed soldiers were everywhere. Red Cross volunteers were everywhere. Lines of lost and looking-for-help people were everywhere. Restless people. Desperate people.

Jade's thoughts went back to what Grandma had once said, "Desperate people do desperate things." *That's probably why there are so many armed soldiers in the Astrodome*, she thought.

As she was inching along in the phone line, she read a large notice on the wall behind the tables: 'NO ALCOHOL. CURFEW – 8 P.M.'

"What does 'curfew' mean?" she asked a young woman who was holding a tiny baby in her arms.

"It means that none of us can be outside the Astrodome after 8 p.m."

"How will they know if it's us walkin' around after eight outside?" Jade asked. She thought she was asking a very intelligent question.

"You're wearing an orange wristband, aren't you? Nobody's going to be wearing long sleeves in this heat. The wristbands will be obvious. You're an evacuee."

Jade had time to think as she was waiting. *An evacuee . . . Why would people need to know we're evacuees? . . . It's enough for us to know that we've lost everything . . . Why do others need to know that, too?*

She remembered reading in *The Diary of Anne Frank* that the Jews had to wear a yellow Star of David on their coats to distinguish them from others. But that was really because the Nazis wanted to get rid of them. *Is the orange wristband on evacuees the same as the Star of David on Jews?* Jade asked herself.

It seemed to Jade that people really wanted to help them.

It was all very confusing.

The young woman wanted to talk, "You didn't ask about the alcohol. If some of the men in this Astrodome got liquor in their bellies, they'd wreck the joint. Men hanging around with nothing to do, believing they've lost everything – family, homes, jobs, places where they were reared – they could go over the edge. Go crazy."

She added as an afterthought, "That is if God isn't strong in their lives."

Jade was feeling sad and scared.

The young woman didn't talk any more.

The line moved very slowly. Jade knew what she was going to ask the young freckle-faced man with curly brown hair, who was working at the phone table.

"Will you be able to call my friend's number, please?"

"Sure thing. Gimme the number."

Jade spat out the number so quickly that the young man said with a laugh, "Now, slow down. Say that again."

It seemed to take an eternity for him to dial the number. Jade noticed he was holding the phone but not talking. He dialled again. Looking at her sympathetically, he shook his head and said, "Sorry. Can't make a connection."

Jade was dumbstruck. Her feet seemed to be Velcroed to the big square in front of the table. When it finally sank in that she wouldn't be talking to Natasha, she pulled her feet up and plodded back to where she had left Grandma and Mary Lou.

"Let's get out into the sunshine. I'd really like to see the showers," Mary Lou said.

She hasn't even noticed I'm sad. She doesn't know how much I'm missing Natasha and my other friends, Jade fumed. She let Grandma push Mary Lou's wheelchair.

When they reached the outside, the dazzling sunshine forced Jade to squint at the large sign pointing to the left: 'SHOWERS'. Following the direction of the sign, they reached heavy plastic sheets attached to metal frames. Shower cubicles. Jade counted ten. Water was running from them down into a street drain.

"Ten showers for fifteen thousand people," Grandma said in disbelief. "Let's ask this Red Cross lady what would be a good time to come in the mornin'."

Marie, the Red Cross lady, said that any time from 5 a.m. would be good.

"I promised to meet Lirette and Brittany at eleven in the foyer to go for Bunty," Jade told Grandma and Mary Lou.

"Maybe we should plan to take showers around eight a.m.?" Mary Lou suggested.

"That's a good time," Jade responded. "If you get up too early all you can do is hang around doin' nothin'." Grandma turned the wheelchair to go back in and Jade helped her to push it.

*   *   *

As they made their way back to their beds through the endless rows, Jade spotted a familiar face, "Summer . . ."

She dropped the handle of the wheelchair and ran over to hug the little girl who had been so ill on the military plane. Summer was sitting, on the edge of her cot, dressing a Barbie doll. She was still very pale and listless so Jade did all of the talking. Summer gave an occasional nod.

"Bunty's outside in the pet place. I'll be goin' over tomorrow mornin' to see her. Would you like to come?" Jade asked excitedly.

Summer nodded, looking shyly at her mother. The little girl's mother had gone over to greet Grandma and Mary Lou. Overhearing Jade's invitation to visit the dog, she asked, "What time, Jade? Summer just loves Bunty."

"At eleven in the mornin'. We're meetin' in the foyer. There'll be two other girls as well." Turning to Summer, Jade said warmly, "You'll like them. They're very nice."

Summer looked over at her mama with a big plea in her eyes.

"Of course you can go over with Jade to see Bunty," her mama said. To Grandma and Mary Lou she added, "I'll never forget you good people. Bunty really helped my little girl. She's improving bit by bit every day. Thank God she's eating now. Think you'll be here long?"

"We're not sure. If my son was here he'd come for us – but he's in Iraq," Grandma replied.

"Lord, you must be worried sick about him. Terrible things happenin' in Iraq. You could say, though, we have our own Iraq here."

"Now you talkin'," Grandma said.

"Will Miss Mary Lou go with you?"

"Yeah. Where one goes all three go," Grandma said looking tenderly at her old neighbour.

"Ah, sure that's great, Miss Mary Lou," Mrs Kingston, Summer's mother, said as she pushed Mary Lou's wheelchair to the side with one hand and with her other hand on Grandma's arm gently pulled her towards her. She talked to Grandma and Mary Lou in a soft voice so that Jade and Summer could not hear what she was saying. When Jade thought the grown-ups were finished and Mrs Kingston was coming back to her daughter's cot, she jumped up from where she had been sitting beside Summer.

"See you in the lobby at eleven, Summer," Jade said as she grabbed the handles of Mary Lou's wheelchair.

Summer's mother, now sitting with her arm around her little girl said "That's nice, Jade. Summer will be there at eleven." Summer nodded but didn't speak.

"That little girl has been through so much, God help her," Mary Lou said sympathetically as they headed to their space at the bleachers.

"Her mama told me she's still worried about her," Grandma added softly.

*   *   *

Later that day Jade went round to visit Summer. She found her wheeling a little doll's pram up one of the narrow paths between the rows of cots.

"Look what I have, Jade," she said, taking a little blonde-haired doll out of the pram and holding it up for Jade to see.

"Nice," Jade said as she began to play with Summer and the doll and pram for a short while. Before returning to her corner, she said, "See you in the morning Summer."

* * *

When Jade told Grandma she had been playing with Summer and that she was talking much more than before, Grandma told her that the little girl's mother had said she was still screaming, "Daddy," in her sleep.

"Po' thing. I'm glad you're looking out for that little girl, Jade," Grandma said gently.

Jade was lying in her cot under the harsh, bright, stadium lights. She could not believe that it was bedtime. Thousands of people were still talking loudly, walking around and shouting at the tops of their voices. But when Jade began to think some happy thoughts about Summer, she drifted off to sleep and dreamed that she and Summer were playing with

Bunty in a beautiful garden with a large lawn and borders of fragrant flowers.

XXI
Mary Lou's Good News

Jade was singing her happy tune as she was making her way to the foyer to meet her friends, "FaldereeEe . . . FalderaaAa." She felt so good since she had showered in the early morning and had washed off a week's grime and sweat. Now her fresh, clean body smelled of lavender.

Summer's mother, Mrs Kingston, was waiting in the foyer with her daughter. Seeing Jade coming through the door, she waved from where she stood near the big noticeboard. It was covered in multi-coloured, large and small pieces of paper, the messages of people looking for family members who had been displaced by the hurricane.

"Hi, Jade," a big smile lit up Mrs Kingston's face.

"Hi," Jade suddenly felt very shy. She quickly looked from the woman to the little girl. Summer's blonde hair was tied up in a ponytail and there was a blush of pink on the tops of her pale cheeks. She looked cute in her red cut-offs and white T-shirt with a yellow smiling face logo. Her blue eyes were brighter than Jade had ever seen before. She could see how much younger Summer was than her new friends and herself as she stood there hanging on her mother's arm, wiggling her right foot at the ankle.

Jade went up to her and said with a big warm smile, "Hi, Summer. That's a cute T-shirt."

"Thank you," Summer said shyly.

Mrs Kingston asked, "Jade, is your neighbour's name, Mary Lou Smith?"

"Yeah. Why?" Jade felt a little impatience. She wanted this time to be girlie time and now Mrs Kingston was here and she was asking about Mary Lou.

Pointing to a big orange poster, hanging crookedly on the end of the message board, she was saying as Jade read, "Mary Lou Smith's nephew, Gary, is looking for her. Call (214) 945-9850," Mrs Kingston added, "That's a Dallas telephone number. Does she have a nephew there?"

"That must be the nephew she always talks about," Jade murmured.

"Maybe your grandmother will call his number to tell him Mary Lou is here with y'all."

Jade suddenly felt cold. *Does this mean that Mary Lou will be leavin' us?* She asked herself.

Just then, Lirette and Brittany arrived. They were excited and a little shy.

"Who are these nice girls?" Mrs Kingston asked with a smile when the bigger girls had said hello.

Jade introduced Lirette and Brittany. Everyone was a bit awkward.

When Jade said, "Let's go get Bunty," Summer let her take her hand.

Mrs Kingston kissed her daughter saying, "I'll meet you back here in half an hour, Summer."

Holding Summer's hand, Jade and the two girls her own age dashed out the door to Bunty.

* * *

Back in the animal enclosure once again, Jade couldn't hold the even more excited jumping, panting, fiff-fiffing Bunty. She leapt and wriggled from her to Summer and back again.

The little girl was smiling as she patted the black and white Jack Russell, who began to cover her face with quick, wet licks, causing Summer to giggle.

"They're Bunty's kisses, Summer. She must really like you," Jade said before she moved away a little bit to let Summer enjoy the dog. She joined the two other girls who were walking other dogs.

When the time in the pet enclosure was up, Jade promised Summer that she'd bring her back again. The little girl gave Bunty a big hug before she left her behind with long backward looks. Jade held her hand.

The four girls walked back to the lobby where Mrs Kingston was standing near the message board.

Summer ran over to tell her mama about her good time with Bunty and how the Jack Russell was pleased to see her.

"That's great, Honey. Did you thank Jade for bringing you to Bunty?"

Turning to Jade, Mrs Kingston said, "Thanks, Jade. You've been so kind to my little girl. I hope everything works out well for you, Grandma and Miss Mary Lou. Oh, don't forget to tell her about her nephew."

Then, giving Jade, Lirette and Brittany quick hugs, Mrs Kingston said goodbye. She took Summer's hand and walked away. The little girl kept looking back over her shoulder. Just as she was going through the double doors into the arena, she waved and shouted, "Bye, Jade."

"Bye, Summer."

Although Jade had known Summer for such a short time, she was like the little sister she never had. Jade felt protective towards her. Maybe that was because she was young and had been so ill. And Summer loved Bunty. The little dog was helping her to get better. Jade told herself, *I'll bring Summer back to Bunty again*.

She was standing lost in her own thoughts when Lirette came over and put her arm around her shoulder saying, "Jade, we're leaving in the afternoon."

Brittany added, "We're also leaving."

Jade was dumbfounded. The new friends she had just made in Houston were going already. *Is life now goin' to be like this? After you make friends, they leave?* Jade thought sadly.

"Thanks, Jade. We loved Bunty. Bye."

All Jade could summon up was a wan smile and after quick, embarrassed hugs, the other two girls ran back into the arena.

Jade took her time and turned towards the noticeboard again. There were so many messages it was difficult to choose where to begin. So many people were like her, lonely and lost. Her heavy heart rooted her to one spot for a while. She began staring trancelike at the colourful messages, thinking about all the people who were missing family members, when suddenly her own name caught her attention: *JADE WILLIAMS . . . Is it true? . . . Am . . . I . . . seein' . . . things?*

186

XXII
Messages on the Bulletin Board

"BERNICE AND JADE WILLIAMS – CALL JORDAN at 1-800-2835768." Jade's heart was thumping. *Uncle Jordan's number . . . Mary Lou's nephew's number . . . We'll be leavin' soon,* Jade thought excitedly as she hopped, skipped and ran back into the arena.

She knew Mary Lou would probably be happy to be going with her nephew. She had said a number of times that she was a burden to Grandma. Jade had grown fond of her and Grandma had said over and over, "Where one goes, all three go." But it was different now.

If Uncle Jordan is comin' for us . . . then it would be nice for Mary Lou's nephew to come for her, Jade thought. *Grandma will call Uncle Jordan . . . Maybe he'll come at the same time as Mary Lou's nephew, Gary . . . Then we'll all be able to leave together.*

When Jade reached the area where the wall jutted out beside the bleachers, Grandma was fixing a white towel over an upside-down crate to make a little table beside her cot. Mary Lou was lying on top of her bed reading a magazine.

Overwrought, Jade exclaimed, "Grandma, Uncle Jordan said call him . . . Miss Mary Lou, your nephew in Dallas is looking for you . . . I couldn't write down the phone numbers . . . They're hanging on the message board in the foyer . . . Isn't your nephew's name Gary, Miss Mary Lou?" Then Jade collapsed on Mary Lou's bed.

Grandma stared open-mouthed. Then she said, "My God . . . Jordan . . . I'm sure he's worried."

Mary Lou sat bolt upright and looked all around as if searching for her nephew, "Where's Gary?" she said.

"There's a number to call him. It's hangin' on the noticeboard in the foyer," Jade was now sitting on the end of her bed, trying to be calm and self-possessed.

Mary Lou's breathing was shallow. She began to wipe the perspiration off her forehead with a small towel that she had beside her. Swinging her legs off the side of her cot, she stood up unsteadily. In a voice quivering with emotion, she said, "God has answered my prayers. I was praying Gary would find me."

Grandma asked, "Did you say the number's in the lobby, Jade?"

"Yeah! . . . On the big noticeboard . . . Ye know the one where the people are looking for lost family members?"

She brought the wheelchair over beside Mary Lou, saying, "Come on, my friend. You have to call your nephew. I have to call my son."

Jade followed Grandma as she pushed her old neighbour towards the foyer, keeping up a conversation about Gary and his wife. She heard that Gary hadn't come visiting for a few years but he did call Mary Lou once a month.

"He was always a good boy," Mary Lou said warmly.

"Grandma, where's Uncle Jordan? Do you think he's home?" Jade couldn't contain her excitement.

"Baby, we'll sure know when we make the call," Grandma said confidently.

"He was always a good boy too," Mary Lou said. "Before he left for the military, he'd pick up some groceries for me if I needed them."

Jade was happy to hear praise for her uncle. He was special to her.

The three of them reached the lobby quickly and Jade guided them, through the anxious, wandering people, over to the noticeboard.

"There they are!" she shouted as she jumped up to point at the two coloured notes.

Grandma reached up to take the two messages off the board, saying, "We'll need these phone numbers." She handed the note from Gary to Mary Lou, putting the other one in her pocket.

"Don't lose Uncle Jordan's, Grandma," Jade warned as they took their place in the phone line.

"No fear, Baby. It's not goin' nowhere."

Soon enough Mary Lou was handed a phone and Grandma and Jade moved up to another free one to talk to Uncle Jordan. They were disappointed to hear that he was still in Iraq, but he did say he would put in a special request to get home as soon as possible.

"That would be great, son," Grandma said, wiping her eyes with the back of her hand.

When Jade saw Grandma crying she couldn't keep her own tears back, so she wasn't able to say very much to her uncle.

"Don't worry, Jade. I'll be home soon and I'll come get you," Uncle Jordan said before he hung up. Jade thought she heard a tremble in his voice.

It was hard to face Mary Lou when they had no good news to tell.

Mary Lou was giggling with excitement, "Gary and his wife are comin' a get me."

"That's good, Miss Mary Lou," Grandma said in a tiny voice.

The three of them made their way back again to their own corner but this time it was different. Mary Lou was elated at the prospect of leaving with her family while Jade and Grandma were feeling sad that she was going and sad too that no one was coming for them.

What about: 'Where one goes all three go?' Jade asked herself angrily.

Although Grandma helped Mary Lou to get her things together and told her she was happy she was going to family, Jade knew she wasn't really happy at all. She looked so sad. She would miss her friend.

When Mary Lou noticed Grandma's sadness, she said, "Dunno how I'm gonna leave you and Jade, Bernice. You've done so much for me."

The three of them gave each other hugs and their tears flowed.

Jade's thoughts went back over that day. A lot had happened. Bad things and good things. It was bad that her new friends had left but it was good to talk to

Uncle Jordan. It was good that Mary Lou had heard from Gary but it was bad that she'd be leaving them to go to Dallas.

The hours before they went to bed passed slowly for Jade. She really didn't want Mary Lou to leave. She couldn't imagine what it was going to be like with Grandma without Mary Lou.

Before she fell asleep, Jade closed her eyes and prayed, *Dear God, please send someone to rescue Grandma and me. Make Miss Mary Lou happy at Gary's. Amen.*

* * *

The next day, around 11 a.m., Mary Lou's nephew and his wife, Kristi, came for her. Jade just couldn't believe that her old neighbour was leaving. After all, Grandma, Mary Lou and she had become like family.

Gary and Kristi sat down beside each other on Grandma's cot while Mary Lou sat beside Grandma facing them on her own cot.

From where Jade stood, she could see Mary Lou's happiness in the pink flush on the top of her cheeks and her eyes dancing with excitement. The old woman talked nervously and even giggled as she recalled going into her good friend Bernice's house to ride out the storm, "Bernice is like my daughter. Jade's the granddaughter I never had."

She went on to tell how she had climbed up into the attic with her neighbour and her granddaughter when the water had rushed into the house.

Jade noticed that Gary, who was staring intently at his aunt as she recalled their harrowing experience, began to look horrified when she described how Bernice and Jade had hacked a hole in the roof with an axe for the three of them to escape from the attic.

But it was when Mary Lou told about being tied with her neighbours to a chimney with an electric cord that tears ran down Kristi's face and Gary jumped up to hug his old aunt saying, "You poor things. If only we'd come sooner."

"If it hadn't been for my dear friends, Gary, I wouldn't have survived," Mary Lou said, fighting a lump in her throat.

Jade's eyes tingled and Grandma bit her lower lip. Gary hugged the two of them. Then sitting down again, he grabbed Grandma's hand in his two hands and pleaded, "Will you and Jade come back with us? We can always make room for you. Let us try to make up for all you've been through."

Where one goes . . . the three will go, Jade was thinking.

"Thanks so much, Gary, but you need to go back with your aunt and spoil her for a while," Grandma turned to Mary Lou, giving her a quick, gentle squeeze, before adding with a nervous laugh, "That'll be a full-time job!"

Jade couldn't push away the sadness. She knew that Grandma was trying so hard to be funny and light. Jade felt heavy and even awkward when she thought that Mary Lou was about to leave them and go to Dallas. She needed to give her a keepsake – but what?

"I'll be back in a minute," Jade said as she rushed over to search on the donations table for some little thing for her old neighbour. She was happy to find a red velvet pillow in the shape of a heart.

When she returned quickly to their corner, she pushed it into Mary Lou's arms, saying gently, "For you Miss Mary Lou." Giving her a warm hug, she added, "Me 'n' Grandma'll miss you."

"I'll miss you too, Jade," the old woman whispered. "I'll never forget your kindness."

Then lifting her big black bag up onto her lap and searching inside, Mary Lou took out her little blue radio and said to Grandma, "Bernice, you could do with this." She blinked back tears as she continued, "You can think of me when you turn it on."

Jade's thoughts went back to the day they had been able to find out about the breach of the levees on the little blue radio when they were in the attic. So much had happened since then.

As Grandma took the radio from her friend, she pressed the $50 bill that the Jewish Rabbis had given her into Mary Lou's hand, saying, "Miss Mary Lou, get somethin' for the three of you to eat on the way to Dallas."

Picturing the bearded strangers who had given Grandma the money when they had visited the Astrodome, Jade began to wonder what had become of them – and the nuns. She had seen so many people come and go since they had come to live in the arena.

Too soon, the time came for Gary and Kristi to leave with Miss Mary Lou. Jade always hated when the time came to say goodbye. It seemed to her that she had nowhere to put her legs and arms so she restlessly shuffled from one foot to the other as she clasped her hands nervously in front.

Grandma handed Kristi two plastic bags full of clothes that she had filled from the table for Mary Lou, muttering something about having some changes for her friend.

Jade hastily hugged Mary Lou and watched as Grandma gave her old neighbour a long, warm, sad hug and murmured, "Stay in touch, Miss Mary Lou." Then she helped her get comfortable in her wheelchair.

Gary began to push Mary Lou as Kristi walked beside him holding Mary Lou's big black bag.

Taking Grandma's hand, Jade had a strange feeling. It was as if she and Grandma were the family walking behind the coffin at a funeral – yet she knew she should be happy for Mary Lou. Her family had come for her. She was a very old woman who needed loving care. She would soon be sleeping in a regular bed in a regular house.

They all reached the outer door of the arena in silence. Jade and Grandma helped to fold up the wheelchair as Gary was buckling his aunt into the back seat of their SUV and Kristi was putting her big black bag and the plastic bags on the seat beside her.

Then Jade and Grandma gave Miss Mary Lou a final hug before the doors were closed, Gary and Kristi slid into their seats in the front and the car eased away from the sidewalk.

When it had turned the corner and they had stopped waving, Grandma slowly led the way back to their place in the Astrodome. She and Jade were in their own worlds of sadness.

"Will we ever see Miss Mary Lou again, Grandma?" Jade asked.

"Only God knows, Baby."

Jade pondered that for a minute or two. She knew she'd miss her old neighbour. Grandma and she were all alone now.

"I just need to rest. Will you be alright for a while?" Grandma said in a low voice as she reached her cot.

Biting back tears, Jade told Grandma that she would be okay.

Grandma got into bed and pulled the bedclothes over her head. Jade felt so alone. Grandma had moved away from her and retreated into her own world. This was the first time Jade had experienced Grandma wanting to shut out the harshness of life. She knew that it would be best to leave her alone for a while. Miss Mary Lou had been her friend and neighbour for many years. She would miss her so much!

Jade decided to make her way through the rows of cots to look for Summer. She had promised to bring her out to play with Bunty and now would be a good time.

When she reached the place where she expected to find the little girl, there was a big empty space. *Maybe I'm in the wrong row*, she told herself as she looked quickly around to check her bearings. *I'd spot Summer anywhere.*

"You lookin' for a small white girl with long blonde hair?" a young dark-skinned woman, rocking a small baby sucking a soother, asked.

Before Jade could answer, she went on, "Cos if you lookin' for her, she left with her family for her Daddy's funeral." And she added gently, "God help her."

Her Daddy's funeral. Jade's heart was now tied in a big black bow. How sad for her new little friend who had been slowly getting back to normal. *Will life ever be normal for Summer? . . . For me? . . . For all of us?*

Muttering, "Thanks," Jade left the young woman and the empty space. She would go out to spend time with Bunty where you didn't have to say a word and you could stay with your thoughts for a long, long time.

XXIII
Soldiers Everywhere

Grandma was stripping Mary Lou's bed when Jade came back into the arena after playing with Bunty. She helped her to fold up her old friend's cot and carry it to the side. When she looked at Grandma's soft round face, she suddenly felt a surge of love for her. Grabbing her in a tight hug, she kissed her cheek. Grandma held her in her soft arms and they slowly sat down on her bed without a word. There was no need for words.

Eventually, Grandma got up saying, "I wanna look for another crate for a bedside table for you, Baby."

Jade followed her over to where she had found the velvet-heart pillow for Mary Lou. She rummaged for other pretty pillows to decorate their beds. She was happy to find a cushion with the word LOVE embroidered diagonally for Grandma and one with a yellow, furry, smiley face for herself. Two multi-coloured throws would help to brighten up their corner and take away the bareness.

"Jade, how about goin' out to McDonald's for lunch when we finish? I've some Red Cross money," Grandma said tenderly with her big warm smile.

Jade felt excited. Going to McDonald's was just like life before the hurricane.

When they had finished their corner, Jade changed quickly into a pair of blue jeans and a pink T-shirt with a sequined swoosh logo across the chest. Then she thought of her lovely silver charm bracelet. She would wear it to McDonald's. Taking it out of its blue box, she said, "It's a pity I have to wear this orange wristband, Grandma," as she began to think of ways to cut it off.

"Jade, don't touch that wristband. You'll need it to get back in here again," Grandma said in her no-nonsense voice.

*　*　*

Jade was thrilled to be doing something as normal as going to McDonald's. She skipped along with Grandma as they left the Astrodome behind and stepped into the hot sunshine. Both remembered having seen a

McDonald's as they drove on the coach into Reliant Park. That seemed years ago to Jade, even though it was less than three days previously.

They turned left out of the Astrodome and kept on walking until they saw the familiar golden arches just a block over. Taking their place in line with ordinary people to place an order, Jade felt as if life might soon become normal again. She ordered a hamburger, fries and a Coca-Cola, as she had done many times before the hurricane. She talked and laughed with Grandma as they tucked into their meal.

When they had finished and were walking out the door, Grandma put her arm around Jade's shoulder saying, "Baby, I'd like to buy you somethin' new to wear."

Jade's heart jumped with excitement. She couldn't remember when she had last got something new. Some of the donated clothes in the Astrodome were cute but they weren't new.

"The server told me that Walmart wasn't too far away . . . She told me how to get there," Grandma said as she began to walk faster. It was hot. Grandma had to slow down a bit until Jade caught up with her. It gave her the chance to mop her brow.

Eventually, they saw a Walmart store and made straight for young fashions. Fortunately, Jade found a top like one of Natasha's and Grandma discovered a pair of shorts to match. Jade thought about her friend and wondered where she was. *Maybe she's in Houston? Wouldn't that be something?*

After they had paid for the new outfit Grandma said, "We need to be getting' back, Baby."

She found it hard to keep up with Jade on the way back to the Astrodome, "Take it easy, Jade. I need to catch my breath."

It seemed to Jade that the distance back to the Astrodome was shorter. When they reached the big arena, they joined a long line snaking into their temporary home.

"It's tough havin' to stand on the cement when my feet be so tired," Grandma muttered as they took up their position on the path outside the double doors leading into the lobby of the huge arena.

"I wonder why we have to line up to get in?" Jade asked Grandma.

A young soldier with a pale thin face was standing nearby and overheard her question. He said in a deep voice, "We have to have strict security here . . . All wristbands must be shown in order to be admitted . . . Bags must be searched . . . Everyone must pass through a metal detector."

Those words struck fear in Jade's heart. It sounded

as if they were being admitted to prison. Soldiers everywhere, special wristbands, a curfew – and thousands of people whose freedom to live ordinary lives had been taken away from them. All of that spoke of prison to Jade.

Grandma's tired voice broke into Jade's thoughts, "Now you have your answer about the orange wristband, Baby."

"Ma'am, show me your wristband . . . Put the bag on the table, please," a young female soldier, her blonde hair tied up under her military cap pointed at Grandma's big holdall.

Grandma put her big brown bag on the table. Jade hoped the soldier wouldn't empty its contents out for everyone to see. *How embarrassin' that would be! . . . You'd never know what Grandma'd have in there.*

But the soldier rifled through the bag quickly and smiled as she gave it back to Grandma. Jade watched Grandma put it down again on a smaller table and walk through what looked like a door frame but was actually a metal detector.

When it was her turn to put her plastic bag with her new purchases on the table for inspection, an overwhelming feeling of annoyance made her slap it down. She didn't even look at the female soldier's pale face. She hated all of this security, especially for her grandmother.

Grandma was waiting for Jade on the other side of the metal detector. People were bustling all around them. So many people had so many questions to ask all of the time. Nobody was sure of anything from one minute to the next.

Eyeing the queue for the phone tables, Grandma said, "I need to try to phone your Auntie Lynn. I'm sure she's worried about us, Jade."

Jade didn't feel like joining another line, so she said, "I'm goin' back. I'll try on my new clothes. Give my love to Auntie Lynn. I'll talk to her again."

Jade rushed back into the arena, walking briskly towards the corner where the wall jutted out from the bleachers. When she was about six cots away, she could see the yellow smiley face on her pillow. It made her feel a bit lighter as she walked. She began swinging the plastic bag holding her new gear.

Grandma and Jade kept their section clean and tidy.

"Baby, this is our home for the present," Grandma had said as she was putting a colourful cloth over a box for her bedside table. "Let's keep it nice. We'll feel better."

Jade knew that she felt much better after putting the love cushion with the red heart on Grandma's bed and the yellow smiley-face cushion on her own.

Changing clothes wasn't what it used to be when she lived in New Orleans. There you could go into your bedroom and close your door. In the Astrodome you had to turn your back on the person nearest you – who could be anybody – and as quickly and discreetly as possible drop your shorts and take off your top. In fact, Jade found it more satisfactory to take off her top first because her new T-shirt was long and then, sitting on her bed, change one pair of shorts for another.

She wondered about Natasha as she pulled the top like her friend's over her head. *If only I could talk to her*, Jade thought.

The wall jutting out from the bleachers offered a little privacy but she always felt as if some stranger was looking at her, no matter how private she tried to be.

"That's nice, love," a woman about the same age as Grandma called out from the side. "You look just like my granddaughter. She's with her daddy in Jackson."

"Thanks," Jade murmured as she folded up the clothes she had taken off and stuffed them under the yellow smiley face. She didn't feel like talking any more. She wasn't really interested in the woman's granddaughter in Jackson.

She decided to walk around in her new clothes before Grandma returned. Heading back up the arena between the narrow rows of cots, Jade turned right to come back again rather than make her way into the lobby. Different people looked at her and some smiled. She passed where Summer's cot had been and wondered about the little girl. *I sure hope she's better*, Jade told herself. She checked to see if the young woman with the baby was there but she didn't see her. *People leave here all the time when their folks find where they are.*

Screams of delight burst into her thoughts and looking in the direction of the excitement, Jade saw two young women and a man hugging and kissing a much older woman.

"Mama, thank God we found you," a young dark-skinned woman with a tidy Afro shouted as she gave the older woman another hug.

As Jade drew level with them, she could see that they were all crying with joy.

"We thought we'd lost ye."

"We've looked everywhere."

"Oh, God! Oh, God. Thank ye, God."

Jade fought back tears. She was happy for those people. But she was sad that no one had come for Grandma and her – yet. She went back to her corner to wait for Grandma.

* * *

"Oh, you're wearin' your new clothes, Jade," Grandma said as she came up to their corner. "Very nice."

"This top's like Natasha's 'member? Wonder how she is," Jade asked wistfully.

"I sure hope she's safe, Baby."

Then Grandma plonked down on Jade's bed and said with a big wide smile, "Jade, I've got good news! Can you guess?"

"We're leavin' here!" Jade shouted excitedly. "Not quite," Grandma said. "But your Auntie Lynn's gettin' an apartment."

A scream of joy exploded from inside Jade at the same time as she sprang up from her cot and landed on the floor. Grandma jumped up too and the two of them hugged and danced on the spot between their cots.

"We'll be leavin'. We'll be leavin'. When is she comin' for us?" Jade asked as she jumped up and down.

"It'll be a little while yet."

Excitement killed. *A little while yet . . . God knows how long that'll be*, Jade thought sadly. She broke away from Grandma and slowly began to take off her new clothes to put on her old ones. Grandma left her alone. When she reflected on it later, Jade thought Grandma must have been disappointed also to have to wait.

Lying down on her cot with her back to Grandma, Jade curled up into a ball and retreated into her own private space.

I CAN'T WAIT FOR ONE MORE THING, she told herself. I'M TIRED OF WAITING!

XXIV
Bunty's Kisses

That night Jade dreamed about Natasha. She could see her looking out the window of a train crowded with people. She waved at Jade, signalling her to come quickly. Jade began to run along the platform to get on the train but the train started to move. It slowly picked up speed.

"Run faster, Jade," Natasha shouted in a high, shrill voice. Jade knew her friend needed her but she was running as fast as she could. At one point she thought she had caught up but the train didn't stop for her to board and it pulled away from her again. Sickeningly, she watched her friend's head and shoulders move farther away, her hand waving frantically as the train sped on.

Finally, Jade had to stop to catch her breath and watch Natasha's waving hand fade into the distance.

She collapsed in a ball of misery, all alone on a deserted platform.

*   *   *

The next morning Jade awakened feeling as if she had been crying the whole night. Her body ached all over. She hadn't changed into her pyjamas so her clothes were now creased and damp with perspiration. Glancing over at the round shape of Grandma, she saw that she had pulled the bedclothes over her head and was still asleep. She wouldn't waken her on her way out to the only friend she had now in the world: Bunty.

Quietly Jade slipped out of bed, put her feet into her flip-flops and made her way down through the rows of cots. Some people were walking around, others were sitting on the edge of their cots and others were still asleep.

Jade felt scruffy. *I'll wash after I've seen Bunty*, she thought.

Mia came to the gate of the enclosure when she saw Jade approaching, "Hi, Jade, you're early this morning."

She was about to say something else when a burst of black and white forced her to step back. Bunty was so excited and Jade soon forgot her sadness in the sheer joy of playing with a little, barking, panting, fiff-

fiffing dog. She knew that she wouldn't swap her dog for anything in the world. Bunty was the best!

When they had run and played, Jade lay down on the grass in the shade of the oak tree, pressing her face into Bunty's back. When she lifted her head, Bunty gave her face quick, wet kisses. That always made Jade smile.

She was feeling much better when she made her way back to Grandma.

"Jade, you haven't washed or changed. Here's some nice soap and a towel. We'll take a quick wash in the Ladies' Room," Grandma said as Jade came up to their corner.

Jade hated washing in the Ladies' Room – a polite name for the women's public toilets. She knew that lining up for a shower was out of the question as it was already late and the queue was winding around the far side of the Astrodome. *It is so embarrassing to have to strip in front of all those women in the public toilets*, Jade fretted.

When they reached the Ladies' Room, the smell of soap, damp towels and perspiration wafted out the door. Some women had stripped to their waists and Jade didn't know where to look. Grandma directed her over to a far corner on the left where there was only one woman.

"I'll stand at your side and no one will see you," she said. "You can do the same for me."

Jade was thinking how lucky she was to have Grandma when she caught sight of herself in the mirror. Two big, sad brown eyes looked back at her. They had seen so many terrible things. Otherwise, she thought she looked much the same on the outside, perhaps a little thinner.

On the inside, she knew she had changed a lot.

* * *

When they returned to their place, Grandma undid some of Jade's cornrows to re-do them. She began to talk about Uncle Jordan and how he had joined the National Guard to get more education, never believing that he would be sent to war in Iraq. "He can't wait to get home. I was tellin' him on the phone that we eat the same MREs as him. He says he's missin' my cookin'." Grandma laughed, "I told him I be missin' my cookin' too. He sends you his love, Jade."

"Did you tell him I sent my love, too?" Jade asked. She just knew that if her Uncle Jordan had been in Louisiana, he'd have come to rescue them.

Then Grandma said, "Auntie Lynn's gettin' her apartment from FEMA, near Jodie, in Baton Rouge."

"Who's Feema?" Jade asked half-heartedly. She hadn't gotten over her disappointment completely.

"Money from the Federal Government for people who suffered in the hurricane," Grandma answered.

"Oh, I thought it was a person," Jade smiled.

Sometime soon . . . HOPEFULLY . . . We'll be stayin' with Auntie Lynn and the boys, Jade told herself.

She lay on her bed telling her self that it wasn't too far-fetched to believe that Auntie Lynn would come in a few days for the two of them. She'd bring them to her new apartment in Baton Rouge. Closing her eyes, Jade prayed, *Dear God, let Auntie Lynn come soon to take us out of here. Amen.*

XXV
Time to go

The next few days in the Astrodome passed in a fog of boredom. What Jade found hardest of all was that she couldn't go outside to play. All she could do was briefly visit Bunty and then help to supervise some of the younger kids in the cordoned-off play area in the arena. She quickly grew tired of that because a number of the young children were sad and cried for no reason. Some didn't want to share their toys and fought over them.

When Jade complained about the kids, Grandma said, "Po' things. Life's rough for them. Help them, Jade."

The truth of it all was that Jade couldn't wait for Auntie Lynn to take them to her new apartment. Eventually came the wonderful and long-awaited moment when Grandma told Jade that Auntie Lynn would be coming for them the next day. *THE NEXT DAY!* Jade was beside herself with joy.

* * *

The next morning she awoke earlier than usual. Her excitement grew when she thought about going to Baton Rouge to live with her two cousins, Jerome aged ten and Steven, who was four years younger. They were good fun. And she really liked her Auntie Lynn.

When she lined up with Grandma for breakfast, Jade felt happier than she had felt for a long time. Even the two middle-aged volunteers from Ohio noticed. The man was juggling fruit and asked Jade to pick a hand from behind his back. She hadn't thought his antics were funny before, but today she laughed when he dropped an apple and made a funny face. The woman laughed and picked it up.

"Good to see you a bit happier today, Honey," said the kind-faced man with a name tag 'Fred'. "I've been worried about you for the past few days."

Maybe it was because she was leaving that Jade began to notice the volunteers. They were ordinary people from all over America and they had come by plane, train, bus and car to help. They did their best to make life a little easier for people like Jade and Grandma, people who had lost everything in the hurricane. Jade felt very grateful. With a big smile she said, "Thanks, Mr Fred."

He replied, "You're welcome, Honey. That beautiful smile makes me happy."

"We're leavin' today, Mr Fred. My Auntie Lynn's comin' for us," Jade enthused.

"Ah, now I know why you're so happy," Fred said as he came around the table to give her a big hug. Choosing two big oranges, he told Jade to keep them for the journey.

Turning to Grandma he said, "I believe people in New Orleans talk about riding out a hurricane when a storm's coming. Three days maybe, huh? This hurricane's a long ride!"

"Now ye talkin', Grandma replied. "Long and rough."

"Glad you goin' to family."

"Yeah! My daughter. Thanks for everything. Hear?"

On the way back to the arena after breakfast Jade heard Jerome before she saw him. A high-pitched "Steeeeven" hit her ears and her heart simultaneously. She ran in the direction of the voice, shouting over her shoulder, "Grandma, the boys are here!"

Jerome was in the children's play area. He had found a guitar and was sitting strumming it as two little girls, aged about three, pressed in for a closer view. Jade arrived in time to see Steven run into the corner, push the children aside and try to grab the guitar off Jerome shouting, "I wanna play."

The boys were too busy wrestling for possession of the guitar to notice that the tall young woman who said firmly, "Give me that guitar before you break it," was their cousin Jade.

By the time Grandma and Auntie Lynn arrived at the scene, the boys were sulking and Jade was handing the guitar to a Red Cross volunteer for safekeeping.

The excitement of Grandma, Auntie Lynn and Jade on seeing each other again washed away any lingering animosity between the boys and Jade. Smiles broke out and laughter rang through the arena. Jade hugged her Auntie Lynn and the boys, telling them how much she was looking forward to living with them in Baton Rouge.

"Have you got all your things?" Auntie Lynn asked in a take-charge voice. "We'd need to make tracks. It'll take us six to eight hours, dependin' on the traffic, to reach Baton Rouge."

"We've put a few things in plastic bags. Jade has her knapsack and I have a big holdall. They're all our worldly goods. It's amazin' how little you can live on," Grandma said softly.

"I need to go out for Bunty."

"Who's Bunty?" queried Auntie Lynn.

"My dog – a little Jack Russell," Jade answered nervously.

"I didn't know you had a dog, Jade," Auntie Lynn said, arching her eyebrows disapprovingly. "The boys have me tortured for a dog but I wouldn't have one about the place."

Icy cold fingers began to play around Jade's heart. She stood riveted to the spot.

"That's a long story about Jade's dog," Grandma interjected. "We'll tell you about it later."

Grandma's matter of fact way of talking about Bunty disarmed Auntie Lynn and eased Jade's tension. She took a deep breath and said, "I'll bring Bunty in."

"Can we come with you?" Jerome asked excitedly.

"Sure," Jade replied.

The boys skipped alongside Jade until they came to the pet enclosure when they gave a whoop and raced for the fence. They knew which dog was Jade's when a blur of black and white hurtled towards her at the gate. They tried to pet the excited, panting, fiff-fiffing little bundle of energy but she had eyes for no one but Jade.

"He won't come to me," lamented Steven, who had gotten into a bad habit, Jade thought, of whining for whatever he wanted.

"It's a she. She needs time to get to know you. When she does, she'll lick the faces off the both of you," Jade told a giggling pair of boys. "But you must be gentle. She doesn't like roughness. She's a lady."

Seeing the wonderment in the boys' eyes, Jade believed that Bunty would have no trouble from them.

She was sorry to have to tell Mia that they were leaving. The young woman had been so kind to Bunty and her during their rough first days in the Astrodome. Even though Mia looked sad when she heard the news, she said she was really glad that they were going to family.

Handing Jade a furry yellow ball with a tail, Mia said, "Bunty loves playing with her toy, Jade. Take it with you and she'll be happy." Then she bent down and wrapped her arms around the dog's neck for a special hug.

Jade hugged Mia and thanked her for all her kindness, telling her she hoped they'd meet somewhere again.

When Jade and the boys got back to Grandma's corner, they found the cots dismantled, leaving a big empty space where they used to sleep.

"Time to go," Auntie Lynn announced. "Help Grandma with the bags, boys. You have enough to do lookin' after the dog, Jade."

"The good people in the kitchen made some sandwiches for us and gave us cold drinks," Grandma said. "I'll hold the plastic bag with the food. Okay?"

People in the surrounding cots shouted their good wishes and told them how lucky they were. One old woman came over to hug Grandma and Jade and to wish them Godspeed.

As they passed through the lobby, Grandma told a Red Cross man that they were leaving. He put his hand in his pocket and pulled out a $100 bill. Giving it to Grandma he said, "I'm happy for you. Get something to eat on the way."

Grandma thanked him and wished him well.

That gesture reminded Jade that, even though some terrible things had happened to them, they had met some really good people.

"God's people are all around," Grandma said as she put her arm around Jade's shoulder. "Baby, God's good. Me 'n' you goin' home."

Jade squeezed Grandma with delight and gave her a big hug. She couldn't wait to be living with Auntie Lynn and the boys.

XXVI
On the Ground Floor

"Put that dog in the back, Jade."

That curt order from Auntie Lynn determined that Jade rode in the third seat of her aunt's station wagon – the seat that faced out the back. The kids called it 'the TV seat' because you are on view to everyone driving behind your car. Jade felt self-conscious sitting on public view but she wanted to make Bunty's journey as smooth as possible. She was sure her little dog knew that Auntie Lynn didn't like her very much. The boys, on the other hand, loved Bunty. They scrambled into the back to be close to her.

While Grandma and Auntie Lynn swapped horror stories about the hurricane, Jade and the boys had fun in the back. They teased Bunty with her toy until she began to bark and Auntie Lynn shouted, "Stop the foolishness."

That's when Jade taught the boys how to play:

I Spy
Hangman
Noughts and Crosses
Fill in the Dots

She felt happy and free with her little cousins, laughing at their antics and their competitiveness.

Time passed quickly and she was surprised when Grandma announced, "We've been drivin' for about two and a half hours. We'd better stop for somethin' to eat."

Auntie Lynn pulled into a Welcome Center. There they ate chicken and tuna sandwiches and drank sodas before tumbling out for a stretch and the toilets. Jade was glad to be able to give Bunty a little run before they all climbed on board again.

The boys fell asleep shortly after that. Jade took Bunty onto her knee and pressed her face into the dog's back. Bunty gave her many wet and sticky kisses.

It wasn't long before Auntie Lynn announced, "We're goin' into Baton Rouge. We'll be at my place in about ten minutes."

Jade could feel her chest getting tighter with excitement and her heart beating so loudly she was sure everyone in the car would hear it. *Soon I'll be in a regular home with my family*, she told herself, giving Bunty a special squeeze that made her little dog look sharply at her. "Sorry Bunty," she whispered. "You know I'm excited."

*　　*　　*

Auntie Lynn stopped the car at an apartment block surrounded by newer, smaller houses, which pressed up against it in a wave of white walls, brightly painted doors and small, tidy lawns. The apartment block stood there like a big, dull brown shoebox amidst the colourful bits of a child's LEGO world.

Jade wondered if the inside of the apartment building was as dull looking as the outside. She would have preferred that Auntie Lynn and the boys were living in one of the more inviting small houses with the brightly painted doors.

Her mind went back to the houses on Seventh Oak Street with their big yards front and back and bright green shutters against gleaming white walls. When she was living there she thought their house was very small. Especially compared with Natasha's! Now, she'd be so happy to walk through the den and make her way into her lovely pink bedroom. Grandma really loved 7 Seventh Oak Street. 'A fine Southern lady,' she called it. *Too bad Hurricane Katrina came*, Jade thought.

"Everyone help with the bags!" Auntie Lynn ordered loudly, waking her two sons from their sleep.

Jade felt sorry for them and helped them to carry two of the bags while she held Bunty awkwardly under her arm. The boys, staggering with sleep, followed their mother, who was opening the main door into the foyer of the apartments.

As she put the little Jack Russell down on the cold tiles, Jade smelled old dust and felt a little chill. The entrance hall was drab and unwelcoming. Someone had hung a framed picture of a faded sunflower on the grey wall to the left of the entrance. On the opposite side, an old poster of a large maple leaf with Canada printed in big red letters was pinned to the wall. The six dark doors off the foyer were closed and looked grim.

"This is our apartment," Auntie Lynn announced as she turned a key in the last door on the right. *At least we're on the ground floor*, Jade thought. *That's good news for Bunty*. She held her breath and looked. It was hard to see into the darkened space before Auntie Lynn turned on the light.

Jade was pleasantly surprised. The den, although hot, was quite big and smelled of new, yellow paint.

Some of the boys' Action Man toys were lying on the floor near the sofa. Auntie Lynn turned on the air conditioning.

"Well, do you like it? Mama, you and Jade can share the boys' bedroom. Steven will sleep with me and Jerome will sleep on the couch," Auntie Lynn said as she opened the door to the right of the den, showing the bedroom that Grandma and Jade would share.

"It's nice," Jade said. *But not as pretty as our home in New Orleans*, she thought.

It didn't take Auntie Lynn long to prepare a meal. Jade smelled the red beans and rice as soon as she walked out of the bedroom, having put her few clothes into a drawer. That's a smell of home, she thought.

When they were eating dinner, Bunty sat begging for something to eat. Auntie Lynn got annoyed, "Jade, put that dog out. I don't like dogs begging at the table when we're eatin'."

"I'll show her the yard," Jerome said, getting down from the table.

Jade followed him. She was sure she could feel Bunty's heart thumping when she held her little pet close. *I hope this isn't a sign of trouble for Bunty*, she thought sadly.

"Dogs are darned nuisances," Auntie Lynn said.

Jade wasn't sure if she was talking about Bunty but she decided to take no chances. She would put Bunty out on the patio at meal times and keep her in her bedroom at other times. She didn't want Auntie Lynn to be able to say that the dog was under her feet. People have a way of exaggerating when they're annoyed.

Grandma told Jade she was wise, "Let there be no rows over a dog in this house."

* * *

Jade began to attend the local public school with Jerome. On her first day she and about fifty other New Orleans kids were called into the gym where the principal and three teachers gave out school supplies, which had been sent to Hurricane Katrina victims from a school in Colorado. They all got a school bag, six hardback notebooks, six pencils, three pens and a ruler each.

How generous those strange kids are . . . I wonder what they heard about the hurricane, Jade thought. She wrote a letter that day during English class to her kind benefactors. She thought they'd like to know that she was now doing okay and that she had a dog named Bunty.

However, things began to change quickly and after a few weeks Jade stopped feeling special. Whenever there was a fight in the schoolyard, the New Orleans kids were blamed. Whenever anything went missing, it must have been taken by a kid from New Orleans. Kids who had been at the school before the hurricane said their school went down when they took in the kids from New Orleans. All of that made Jade very unhappy. She wanted to leave that school.

She only felt a little better when she was day-dreaming about the teachers and her friends in St Albert's and telling herself she'd be back there soon. She thought about the smart kids in her New Orleans school – like David Seemore. *What had happened to David? . . . And no teacher in this school in Baton Rouge can compare with Mr Cooper . . . What about him?*

Mr Cooper's home was in Chalmette. Jade knew that the water had gone to the roofs of the houses in Chalmette. *Did he evacuate in time?* She hoped with all her heart that he was safe somewhere.

And Natasha . . . What had happened to her? Jade pictured petite, pretty Natasha dressed in her shimmery burgundy and grey cheerleader outfit, springing lightly up on her knee and then onto her shoulders in the pyramid. *Hold 2, 3, 4 – down – spreadeagle jump – high – shake pom-poms . . . Cool.*

Natasha and Jade, directly in front of the band, marching with the cheerleaders in St Albert's Mardi Gras parade. Everyone laughing. Happy.

Were Natasha and her family rescued? . . . They probably were! Jade thought reassuringly.

* * *

One Saturday afternoon Auntie Lynn and the boys had left for football practice and Jade was sitting beside Grandma, with Bunty on her knee, watching TV.

Suddenly Grandma said with a serious face, "Jade, I've somethin' to tell you."

Jade stiffened, bracing herself. She always knew by Grandma's face when she had something unpleasant to say.

"We can't stay here," Grandma said abruptly.

It took a minute for the shock of what Grandma had said to register with Jade before she responded nervously, "What do you mean, Grandma?"

"Baby, Auntie Lynn got the apartment rent-free from FEMA for three months. The time'll be up soon. She'll have to find another place here in Baton Rouge. Anyway, I'd like to go back to New Orleans."

"How can we go back, Grandma? Isn't everywhere flooded?" Jade snapped. Her head was pounding. Her ears wanted to shut out what Grandma was saying. "What did you say FEMA was?"

"FEMA's the Federal Government's Emergency Management Agency. The government's giving trailers rent-free if your house got damaged by the hurricane. I took the number down from the TV and I'm goin' to apply for one."

Jade was silent. Grandma continued with a gentle coaxing voice, "We'll have our own place, Jade. You'll be able to have a bedroom of your own again. Wouldn't that be nice?"

It would be nice to have a room to myself, Jade thought. *I don't have anything against Grandma . . . but . . . I don't have privacy here . . . And she likes to take a nap in the afternoon . . . It would also be great to leave this school . . . But I'll miss Auntie Lynn and my cousins.*

These thoughts raced through Jade's mind, bumping into each other and making so much noise she had a hard time hearing Grandma.

"I had a call from Zack askin' if I'd go back to work in the restaurant. He wants to open up as soon as possible to help to get the people back to the city . . . Baby, I wanna work . . . This hangin' around ain't no good . . . You get lazy . . . And the money's good."

Jade's head was buzzing with the weight of Grandma's words and her own thoughts. She was feeling torn. Life had been normal in Baton Rouge for such a short time. She liked living with her cousins. Okay, they could get on your nerves some times but they were only young kids and could be good fun.

But then there was school. The thought of the possibility of going back to St Albert's gave Jade an instant lift.

And what about Bunty? Where I go, she goes.

"Baby, when the insurance money comes through for 7 Seventh Oak Street we can get the house fixed and move back home. But before that, we'll be livin' in a trailer."

A trailer. We'll be livin' in a trailer, Jade repeated over and over.

"Where will the trailer be, Grandma?" she asked when she had found her normal voice again.

"I'm puttin' in for one nearest our old neighbourhood," Grandma answered.

* * *

From that day, Grandma talked much more about returning to New Orleans. Jade began to feel happier about moving too. She was particularly glad when she found out that they'd only be about an hour's drive from Auntie Lynn and the boys.

It wasn't too long before a letter came in the mail for Grandma. It was an official letter from FEMA telling her that she had been allocated a trailer in Melross State Park, across the Mississippi River on the West Bank. Although Jade knew that New Orleans was on the two sides of the river, she had never before crossed the Mississippi River Bridge to the other side.

"That's very far away, Grandma," she said.

"Not really. You can take a shortcut. Cross the river by ferry."

"Really?" Then Jade asked Auntie Lynn, "What'll it be like living in a trailer?"

"Like a regular house. A tinchy-winchy one."

Jade couldn't imagine anything smaller than the house she lived in with Grandma. Auntie Lynn had spent a holiday in a trailer in Destin, Florida. If she says 'tinchy-winchy' then she knows, Jade thought. Small, very small!

Auntie Lynn got out a map to let Grandma and Jade see where they would be living. She was able to figure out that Melross State Park was about twenty minutes from their old neighbourhood, if they travelled over by ferry.

After that day, Grandma was so happy that she sang some of her favourite jazz songs as she moved around the apartment. The song she particularly liked was a

New Orleans favourite, 'When the Saints Go Marching In'.

"That be talkin' about us movin' back home," she told Jade one day, in her get-down-Baby-voice, swaying to the music. Her enthusiasm was infectious and Jade joined in the chorus, sashaying and singing:

> . . . I wanna be in that number,
> When the saints go marchin' in.

* * *

At last, the day for their departure arrived. Jade spent all morning arranging and rearranging her clothes in a brand new suitcase that Auntie Lynn bought for her. She also put the finishing touches to the 'Thank You' card she was making for her, Jerome and Steven.

When Grandma had packed her clothes, she helped Lynn to make sandwiches for a picnic. The journey would be much shorter than from Houston to Baton Rouge but Grandma knew that everyone loved a picnic. Jade helped by getting the two litre bottles of Coca-Cola and Root Beer out of the fridge and putting them into one of the picnic bags.

Climbing into the station wagon with Grandma, Bunty, Auntie Lynn, Jerome and Steven, Jade didn't care that she was riding in the TV seat. She couldn't wait now to see her new home.

When the boys asked where she'd be living, she told them her new address would be a trailer in Melross State Park.

"I know that sounds strange," Jade said, "It'll be home until 7 Seventh Oak Street gets fixed up."

XXVII
The Boys Stopped Playing

Jade wasn't prepared for it. She couldn't believe what met her eyes when the car rounded the corner of Melross State Park. There were hundreds and hundreds of identical large white boxes in straight rows, gleaming in the sun. Trailers. Her heart sank and she could hear Grandma let out a deep sigh.

"Is this it?" Jade asked nervously.

"Yeah. This is it for the present. Until we can get back into our own house, Jade."

Auntie Lynn stopped the car in the only open space available in the field where the trailers were stuffed into parallel lines. Nobody got out of the car. It was as if they were all wrapped in a soft blanket in the car. Outside, the winds were blowing harsh and strong.

A trailer marked 'OFFICE' was standing alone at

the edge of the space. Its white exterior looked blue with cold.

"Are you sure you want to stay here? You can always come back with me," Auntie Lynn said in a voice just above a whisper as she surveyed the white landscape crammed with trailers.

Jade held her breath. All at once she was awash with fear. Maybe it would be a good idea to go back with Auntie Lynn before they stepped out of the car.

"We're here for now, Lynn," Grandma said. "I have to check at the office to see where we're goin'." Grandma opened the car door and swung her legs out the side before she stood up. Then she walked towards the office.

Jade's heart was in her mouth. She had worried about being able to find their corner in the Astrodome but this would be much harder, she thought. And the trailers were packed so tightly together, she would be afraid of letting Bunty go out without a leash in case she'd lose her little hurricane dog.

Tumbling half-heartedly out of the car, Jade and Jerome followed Grandma into the office where a balding man with a red face sat behind a desk stacked with papers. He looked at them over his glasses, which had slid to the end of his nose.

"What can I do for you?" he said with a smile, fingering a letter and glancing from it to Grandma.

"I have a letter from FEMA sayin' I have a trailer here," Grandma said nervously.

"Let me see," the official said.

The man read the letter that Grandma had given him. Then he handed her a key saying, "Number 299. Will you be able to find it yourselves? I'm on my own here."

"Oh, yeah," Grandma said, sounding relieved as she took the key.

"Everything should be in order, Ma'am."

"Thanks."

"You're welcome."

Jerome pushed out of the office ahead of Grandma. By the time she had emerged into the glaring sunshine and had slowly come down the steps, Jerome shouted, "Look, there are sticks with numbers painted on arrows: 100, 200, for the rows of trailers. Let's go down row 200." He and Steven ran ahead with a panting Bunty on her leash and a breathless Jade taking up the rear.

They stopped in front of a trailer with '#299' in the window. The one good thing was that it was at the end of a row, near an azalea bush. Jade's thoughts went back to the azalea in the back garden of 7 Seventh Oak Street. Maybe having one growing near their new home in Melross was a good omen.

"Here it is," Jerome shouted triumphantly, running up the steps to open the door of trailer 299, which was locked.

Jade signalled back to Grandma and Auntie Lynn, who were a good bit behind carrying bags and the key, that they had found the right one. She was now so excited that she found it hard to wait.

When the two adults joined them a minute or two later, Grandma opened the door into the main living area containing a couch, dinette and small kitchen. Everything was compact and smelled new. *The whole trailer is the size of our living room in Seventh Oak Street*, Jade thought.

The boys rushed ahead into the bedroom on the right and jumped onto a queen-sized bed, which filled up the whole room. "This is Grandma's," they announced as they sprawled on top of it.

The tiny kitchen – complete with refrigerator, cooker, sink and microwave – fascinated Jade as she explored everything. She walked down the narrow hall leading to the bathroom with its mini-shower and sink. It was hard to believe that their home was now this weekend travel trailer going nowhere.

"Here's my room," she shouted when she found the small room at the back with four bunk beds. "Look Jerome 'n' Steven. You can sleep here when you come."

When they had finished examining everything, all five of them squashed into the dinette corner to eat the sandwiches Grandma had put on little blue plates from the kitchen cupboard. Jade thought it was just like playing in a toy house. She loved it.

"Aren't we lucky, Grandma?"

"Yeah, so lucky . . . Blessed I'd say . . . And I've no rent or utility bills to pay . . . Some wonderful angel's left everything ready for us . . . Think of it . . . Beds made, towels in the bathroom and food in the ice box . . . God's good," a smiling Grandma said.

Taking a large bottle of Coca-Cola out of the refrigerator, Grandma poured everyone a drink in plastic cups she had found under the sink. They all enjoyed the sandwiches and drink.

After a minute or two Auntie Lynn said, "Time to go. Sorry for eatin' 'n' then leavin' but we'd better get on the road." Then looking around the small area where they were seated, she said enthusiastically, "I like this! You'll be happy here and you're not too far away. I suppose you'll be goin' to school—"

"Now, wait . . . We're only here," Jade cut in.

Auntie Lynn didn't pursue the matter and grabbed her things, saying, "Come on, boys. Time to go."

As she hugged her aunt and the boys before they departed, Jade felt sad. It was strange waving goodbye to them and then being left alone with Grandma in something like a toy home.

"Jade, let's put our clothes in our wardrobes," Grandma said cheerily as she went back up the steps of the trailer.

As she was putting her few things away, Jade thought that there was enough room in her bedroom for Natasha if she ever decided to visit them in Melross Park.

When she returned to the den, the television was on in the corner. Bunty began to bark near the door so Jade said, "Grandma, Bunty needs to get out for a run. I'll keep her on her leash."

Jade looked at the small pink azalea bush near the trailer as she went down the steps into the bright sunshine and turned left. The azalea would be the marker for their new home, which looked just like all the rest. A shiny white box.

She walked up the narrow, grassy path between the trailers, feeling the burning heat reflecting off their aluminium sides. The path appeared to go on forever. It seemed to Jade that the trailers were all strung together with electric wires like giant skipping ropes. A big white pipe anchored each trailer into the ground like a thick circular root. A gas tank was connected to each trailer.

Jade had a strange feeling as she walked with Bunty. So many trailers on top of each other and no life. *Where are the children?* Not one was to be seen. All the identical doors were firmly closed. *Maybe we're among the first to arrive here*, Jade thought.

It took her a long time to reach the end of row 200 because Bunty had to sniff the base of all the trailers. "Come on, Bunty. You don't need to smell everything," Jade said impatiently as she turned the corner at the end of their row and pulled the dog along with a little jerk on the leash.

Just then, she heard the excited squeals of children playing. In a small clearing, she could see young boys playing football. A much bigger kid, leaning on a crutch with his back to Jade, blew a whistle as Jade was walking up. The boys stopped playing and he called them over to him.

XXVIII
A Change in David

"Careful now. Don't knock me down."

There was something about the way the big boy held his head at an angle and said those words that was familiar to Jade. The way he held his head. The voice. *Could it be? Ah, no! Could it really be?*

"David," Jade rushed towards him and threw her arms around his neck.

Dropping his crutch, David grabbed Jade and swung her off her feet saying, "Jade, where did you come from?"

The young boys began to giggle. Turning towards them David said, "Guys, go 'n' play." Then grabbing Jade's arm, he steered her towards a set of steps to a trailer near them and sat down with her. "Jade, I've been trying to find you," David said excitedly as he straightened out his right leg on the steps.

"I've been wonderin' about you too, David," Jade said, turning her body around to look at him directly.

"Are you living in this trailer park now?" David asked, his eyes dancing all over Jade's face. "I'm in number 15 with my Mama and my sister."

"We just came here today," Jade answered. "We're in number 299. Weren't you in your grandmother's for the hurricane?"

"Yeah, only until Sunday morning when the mayor gave a mandatory evacuation order. We left in two cars for our cousins outside Baton Rouge."

"I ended up in Baton Rouge too," Jade interrupted excitedly.

"Really. Did you go straight there?"

"No. We were on the roof and on a bridge," she paused and added darkly, "Hell."

"Oh my God."

That was how Jade began to tell David the horrors of what had happened to her and how David told about moving on from Baton Rouge to Shreveport when his mother's money ran out.

"What happened to your leg, David?" Jade asked, trying to be normal. David's face clouded over when he told Jade how he had torn some ligaments jumping down from a wall near a shelter in Shreveport when a gang surrounded him demanding money.

"That's terrible," Jade sympathised.

"Yeah. What happened to me was bad – but it wasn't as bad as what happened to Mr Cooper."

"What happened to Mr Cooper?" Jade asked, suddenly feeling tightness in her chest.

"I heard somewhere that he was rescuing people in a small boat when a huge section of roof fell on him. It broke his legs and his pelvis. I believe he's in a hospital in San Antonio."

Jade felt that she didn't want to hear another bad thing in this world ever again. She heard herself saying, "That's desperate, David. He was such a good teacher."

"Yeah, I really liked him. I hope he'll be okay," David said sadly.

Jade and David stared into the distance for a few minutes through a heavy net that had suddenly dropped around them, imprisoning them in ghastly memories.

"Have you heard about anyone else?" Jade enquired. "I tried to call a few people when I was waitin' to be rescued. You. Dwight. Natasha. Have you heard anything about Natasha? I couldn't make contact with anyone after the first day or two."

David sucked his lower lip and said, "I don't know how to tell you this, Jade."

Jade hated when anyone said that to her. Her heart dropped inside her body. She prepared herself for the worst by holding her breath for too long and then gasping, "What?"

It seemed like an eternity before she heard something that sounded like, "Natasha's gone."

"Gone where?"

"Dead."

"DEAD?"

All at once Jade was locked with shock. She was almost mad with it. She could feel the colour drain out of her face. A cold dampness began at the roots of her hair. It crawled down her face, neck, body and out into her hands. She felt that she had melted down into a lifeless wet blob. *Did he say Natasha's dead?* She asked herself with deep dread. *Dead? Natasha's dead?*

From somewhere beside herself, she heard a hollow voice asking, "What happened?"

"She drowned. The veranda – the one outside the bedroom – collapsed. She fell into the water."

David held his face in his hands and with quivering lips whispered, "She never came up."

Jade lowered her head onto her knees and put her two damp, cold hands over her ears as she tried to get her head around what David had just said. *Drowned . . . But not Natasha . . . It couldn't be . . . She's a great swimmer*. Then a terrible thought pushed its way into Jade's mind. *Natasha talked about seein' alligators . . . in the water . . . in a lake near her home. Ugh!*

Drowned.

Dead.

Alligators.

A searing pain ripped through Jade's heart. She just couldn't believe her best friend was dead. She felt David's arm around her shoulders. He was on his knees murmuring, "Sorry. Sorry. I know she was your best friend."

Pulling Jade close to him, he said with sadness, "I really liked her too."

Jade didn't want David to see her break down. She couldn't let a boy see her crying. A force outside herself pulled her away from him. Holding Bunty's leash, she half-fell, half-ran down the steps of the trailer.

RUN . . . RUN . . . RUN . . .

XXIX
A Sign on a Porch

Jade ran and ran. She ran as fast as she could, the small dog at her heels trying to keep up. She ran past line after line of trailers, the dust pounding, the breath catching in her throat, until she spotted the familiar azalea bush. She fled for the safety of their trailer, pulling open the door and rushing in. She ignored Grandma as she threw herself against her bedroom door and flung herself onto the bunk.

"What's the matter, Jade?" Grandma called out with concern as she fled through the small den. "What is it?"

"Leave me alone," Jade shouted into her pillow. She didn't want to talk to Grandma. She didn't want to talk to anyone! "Leave me alone," she shouted again.

Rolling over onto her side, she pulled the patterned quilt up around her shoulders, feeling suddenly cold. "Natasha . . . Natasha . . . Natasha . . ." she said her friend's name over and over again. Not wanting to believe what she'd heard. Not wanting to think that so many bad things had happened in her own life.

So many bad things. *No daddy . . . Mama dyin' when I was born . . . Grandpa got sick and died while Grandma was workin' two shifts in Zack's to help pay for the hospital bills . . . I loved Grandpa even if he was grumpy like Grandma said when she was mad with him . . . My family's fallin' apart. Uncle Jordan off fightin' with the National Guard in Iraq . . . Auntie Lynn and the boys stayin' in Baton Rouge . . . Even Mary Lou who cared for me since I was small, gone to live with her nephew in Dallas . . . I might never see her again.*

Emotion overwhelmed Jade as she remembered all that was lost. Thousands of people lost their homes and their families, waiting for days for help in the awful heat and dirt, on the bridge and outside the Convention Center. The old lady she never knew who died in her wheelchair in the burning heat. A dead man floating face down in the polluted water. People's furniture, pictures, keepsakes and clothes – all swept away. Mr Cooper lying ill in some hospital and

NATASHA DEAD. So many bad things had happened since the hurricane.

How many bad things can a person suffer? Jade asked herself as her heart broke into a million pieces, falling to the bottom of a deep well of all the tears she had shed since the beginning of the storm. She cried and cried till a heavy aching tiredness overcame her and dragged her into a fitful sleep.

When she awoke it was dark outside. Grandma was sitting on the edge of the bunk. "Your friend David came by to see you," she said softly. "He told me about Natasha . . . I'm sorry, Baby, so sorry. I know how close you two were and what a good friend she was . . ."

"The best," Jade whispered, words sticking at the back of her throat.

"Losin' someone you love is hard, the hardest thing to happen to a person in their lifetime. I know how much you will miss her now that she's gone."

Grandma's soft, kind words only opened the sluice gates of Jade's tears again. "I . . . don't . . . want her . . . to be gone," she managed to stutter amidst aching sobs. "I want her to phone me . . . to text me . . . to talk to me. I need to hear her voice."

She reached for her phone to replay Natasha's message from weeks back asking her about some maths homework and wondering who they both thought was the hottest boy in class.

Jade melted into a sea of sadness, at one with her dead friend.

Grandma said nothing. She just sat there for the longest time, holding Jade's hand in hers as they both listened to Natasha's voice over and over again until Jade's sobs weakened and finally stopped, her body becoming still.

"You're lucky you can listen to Natasha's voice, Jade. Lord, how I miss your Grandpa's voice," Grandma said. "Wish I'd a phone like that to help me remember the sound of it."

* * *

When David came home from school, he knocked on the trailer door to ask Jade to come out for a walk. As they walked down the narrow path between the trailers, he didn't mention anything about Mr Cooper or Natasha but talked about school.

Jade told him she was nervous about going to another school. She didn't know any of the kids. She was worried that she wouldn't make friends easily.

David told her not to worry. "I'm there, Jade. You already have a friend," he said, a big warm smile lighting up his big dark eyes and playing around his mouth. "A bus will pick us up at the entrance to the trailer park every day."

But I've lost my BEST friend, Jade told herself. *Has he forgotten so soon?*

She tried to be interested in what David was saying but she pulled all of herself inside, the way a snail retreats into its shell when anyone touches it.

They didn't spend long together.

* * *

That evening, when Grandma and Jade were eating the Gumbo Auntie Lynn had made for them, Jade told her what David had said about school. Grandma said that she had put her name down when they came to Melross and she'd be starting the following week.

Annoyance flared up in Jade. "When were you goin' to tell me about my own life?" she shouted. "Grandma, I hate the thought of goin' to another school."

"Baby, you'll be okay. I didn't talk to you about it before now. You just needed a bit of time for yo'self. Yo' lucky havin' a friend like David there."

A friend like David? . . . He's not Natasha, my BEST friend . . . Grandma should understand . . . I just don't get over Natasha's death that easily.

Grandma could see some of Jade's pain and left her with her thoughts.

David says the new school's nice. The teachers 'n' kids are kind to the New Orleans evacuees. Some of them had to evacuate themselves but feel lucky that they got back into their own homes which weren't destroyed.

After some time, having sat at the table in silence, Grandma got up to wash a few dishes saying, "Baby, I need to get back to Zack's . . . now that we have a place. D'ye know . . . I heard they lettin' us go back to look at our homes . . . Maybe the two of us could take a look at 7 Seventh Oak Street."

When Jade didn't respond, Grandma asked, "What d'ye think?"

Jade thought about it. "When?"

"Why not tomorrow?" Grandma replied. "A minivan leaves from Melross at noon."

"Okay, Grandma," Jade said without any feeling. She didn't much care what they did, provided she didn't have to go to school straight away.

* * *

The next day, Grandma and Jade were sitting in the back of a minivan being driven across the Mississippi River Bridge into the business district of New Orleans.

"Why are we goin' the long way, Grandma?" Jade asked. Earlier, she had perked up a bit thinking that the van would drive onto the ferry for the journey across the Mississippi.

"The ferry's out o' commission since the storm, Baby. I sure hope it gets fixed soon. I'll need to be takin' it for work," Grandma answered.

Jade was shocked to see the hurricane damage as they drove along. All the windows that had been blown out of the Hyatt Regency Hotel by the ferocious winds. She had seen the pictures on TV but she told Grandma, "To see this with your own eyes is different."

Further along, the driver had to stop at a military checkpoint. He showed a letter saying that he was driving passengers to look at houses in the Ninth Ward and was allowed to proceed.

Jade was forced to take a big long gasp of horror when her eyes roamed over the barren landscape as they drove into the Ninth Ward. They drove along a main road that had been cleared of fallen trees and debris from buildings that had collapsed. Torn curtains were blowing out through jaws of fractured glass in houses that were still standing – their front doors lying open – but uninviting.

Uprooted trees were sprawled across the side streets and buildings, their limbs mangled in electric wires, a grim reminder of the fury of hurricane winds. Everything was so strange in this moon-dust barrenness. There were no people. There was no life. Everything was covered in a thick, brownish-grey dust. The surface of an alien planet that was once home.

Colourful soft toys tied to a sign on a porch of an abandoned house caught Jade's attention. She read, *Bye N'Awlins. We loved ya!* Sadness washed over Jade. *Where are the children who used to play with those toys now?* She wondered.

The minivan stopped at the bottom of Seventh Oak Street. A path had been cleared through the silt, downed trees, wrecked buildings and trash, for people to make their way on what had been a regular street. Jade and Grandma set off in the direction of their old home.

Jade's dazed eyes followed a sea of wreckage. She looked for landmarks and at first saw none, but as soon as her mind adjusted to the devastation, she began to pick out the ruins of familiar buildings.

The tin roof had been blown off the washateria at the corner of Seventh Oak Street and Pine. Every window had been blown out in the Pittmans' house, one of the few two-storey houses in the street. The wall was missing on one side, exposing what had been a bathroom on top of the kitchen. Jade wondered what their own house would be like.

An eerie silence lay over the blighted neighbourhood as Jade walked up the street ahead of Grandma. She stopped in front of 7 Seventh Oak Street.

XXX
WE Can Only Look Today

Jade stood immobile as she looked at their house on Seventh Oak Street.

She felt as if she was looking at one of the brown and grey raggedy pictures from long ago that Grandma kept in a tin box at the top of the wardrobe. Something vaguely familiar, yet old and battered.

The once gleaming white exterior was now an ashen grey. The green paint was peeling off the closed shutters and a brownish-black grime-line ran along the front of the house above the window.

"Grandma, look at that dirty line all the way round the house," Jade said softly when she eventually found her voice.

"Yeah. The mark left by the stinkin' floodwater,"

Grandma said in a low voice, her face expressing all of her concern.

"Ugh," Jade shuddered. "It's over my head."

Jade thought about that – *Over my head!* – and she shuddered again.

"And the big X near the door?" she asked in a whisper.

"The rescue workers woulda left that when they searched the house. They made an '0' in the bottom part of the X when they found no dead bodies," Grandma answered, pursing her lips and shaking her head.

Shivers ran down Jade's spine as she thought of all the dead people she had seen since the hurricane. The man lying face down in the filthy, smelly, oily water with trash floating all around him when Grandma, Mary Lou and she had been rescued off the roof by boat. The woman who fell to her death with a hair-raising scream when the house split in two. The old woman who died outside the Convention Center and whose family had to leave her in her wheelchair covered in a sheet.

And then there was Natasha. Drowned. Jade felt sick to her stomach. So many people dead, including her best friend.

Slowly her weary eyes examined the grey caked mud in the wreck of the front garden. She recognised a familiar shape lying in the debris between an old piece of awning and a rusted lawnmower.

"Grandma, there's my teddy," she said as she walked towards the teddy she'd had since she was a baby. Its head, showing its loved-into-baldness patch, lay at the wheel of the lawnmower and its body, dressed in baggy dungarees, was caught under a rusted, mangled strip of metal.

Grandma pulled Jade back saying, "Baby, we can only look today. Everything full o' disease. We can't touch nothin'."

Then she began to root in her holdall and taking out two plastic white masks she said, "Jade, put that on. I shoulda give you one sooner."

Putting the mask over her nose and mouth only added to Jade's feeling of strangeness. An alien in her own neighbourhood.

"I wanna take my teddy home to give him a good washin'," Jade said in a muffled voice, her breath bouncing back hot from the plastic mask.

"I know, Baby, but that's too dangerous. Your health's more important."

Jade felt empty. Stripped. *So I won't be able to take my teddy? And my special things? It isn't fair.* She wasn't able to take them with her when they had to climb into the attic when the floodwater was rising in the house. Anyway, she didn't have any room in her knapsack.

"We sure made a big hole to get out on the roof," Grandma said with a nervous laugh.

Jade's teeth began to chatter. She suddenly felt that the sun had darted behind heavy black clouds and the temperature had dropped to freezing point.

When her eyes caught sight of Grandma's mangled car under the collapsed carport, stuck between two uprooted trees, she grabbed Grandma's arm and pointed.

"Yeah, the old Chevy's a goner," Grandma said gently. "But it served us well. We've a lot to be grateful to God for, Jade. Our house – the only one standin' tall in the whole block – 'n' look at us! We've come through a lot."

Grandma's words helped Jade to calm down. Yes, their house was the only house that wasn't badly damaged on the outside. True, the carport had been ripped off the side of the house, but apart from the hole in the roof that they had made themselves, the house had no other exterior damage.

Looking over at Mary Lou's side of the house, Jade thought about her old neighbour and wondered if she'd return to see the house. Grandma must have read Jade's thoughts.

"What a pity Miss Mary Lou can't see how her house has weathered the storm so well. I wonder if Gary will bring her back to take a look," she said wistfully.

The image of Mary Lou lying outside the Convention Center on a piece of cardboard flashed into Jade's mind. *I thought she would die there*, she told herself.

"What a shame Miss Mary Lou isn't here with us," Jade whispered sadly.

Grandma's soft arms pulled her close, showing her that she knew and understood. "Better for Miss Mary Lou to be with her own family now, Jade," Grandma said softly.

Gently nudging Jade forward and in a forced happy voice she added, "Let's take a look inside."

They walked carefully up the steps of the porch, their feet crunching on baked mud that looked like a brown clay mosaic. Grandma's plants and flowers were all washed away. Jade pulled open the green shutters to enable the both of them to peer through the window into the den.

"Oh, Grandma!" Jade was shocked at what she saw. She put her arm around her grandmother's slumped shoulders as they both looked at the mess in their home.

Every bit of furniture and all their possessions were destroyed, like someone had poured some weird kind of chocolate fudge over everything. She could only guess how bad it must smell when she thought of what she had seen floating in the water. There was nothing worth saving. The table, the chairs, the big comfy sofa, the dresser, everything was just one big sludge heap in the middle of the floor. Even the TV lay turned over, smashed and broken like a soda can.

Jade's eyes roamed up the blackened, mouldy walls to the painting of Mardi Gras masks that Grandma liked so much. A sooty film covered the once bright yellow, green and purple feathers, making them look like filthy dish rags.

Jade looked away quickly but not before she noticed that all of the family pictures were gone from the wall near the kitchen door. Grandma's wedding picture and her Kindergarten Graduation picture. Gone! Probably lying somewhere in the muck.

"Oh, Baby, how will we ever get this place cleaned up? Look where the fridge landed. And look at your lovely bed."

Jade could see the fridge lying on its side in the den, next to the sofa. On top of the sofa sat the kitchen table, its buckled, warped legs in the air. *But where is my bed?* Then she saw the pink metal headboard with the two hearts cut out of the middle. It had become disconnected from the rest of the bed and was lying near the sofa. At the bedroom door, she could see a mucky mattress on the floor.

"Oh, God. I be too old for all this, Jade. I won't be able to get this house fixed."

Jade, too, was thinking, *Yeah, this house is gone. Life here is over.*

She tightened her arm around Grandma's shoulder and the both of them were silent in the face of the devastation.

Then from somewhere inside herself, Jade pulled on a reservoir of strength. She pushed the upset at the sight of her sodden collapsed bed, its beautiful pink cover now filthy brown, from her mind. She pushed away too the realisation that everything she owned, her baby pictures that Grandma had given her in a special album on her birthday, her Kindergarten Graduation picture, her jewellery and her cheerleader outfit lay buried in the stinky, mucky grave of their home.

"Grandma, we can do this," she whispered. "We can. I'll help you. Remember, we're in this together. We can fix up the house. Get new furniture, new beds. Do the garden."

Those words seemed to touch Grandma deeply and tears began to run down her face. Jade rustled in her pocket for a tissue but couldn't find one. She took her arm from around Grandma's shoulder and pushed her hand up her sleeve to find a crumpled unused one. She dabbed it at Grandma's eyes.

Taking the tissue, Grandma blew her nose and took a deep breath. She seemed to be lost in her own thoughts for ages. Jade was wondering if indeed Grandma and she could straighten this house up when Grandma turned towards her, her eyes looking scared. Then she pulled herself back from a distant place and with her jaw set at the determined angle that Jade knew so well, she said the words that Jade so desperately needed to hear, "Right, Jade. We're in this together. We can't give up now. God will give us all the strength we need."

They grabbed each other in a big hug that lasted a long time until Jade pulled on a special memory of New Orleans as she whispered gently to the older woman, "And the people will come back, Grandma. N'Awlins is a special place. People say there is nowhere else like it in the world."

Grandma slipped her arm into Jade's as they both stood close together, lost in thought for a few minutes, looking at their home. Then they turned slowly to retrace their steps, back out through the garden to the sidewalk.

Jade glanced back at the house. This time she saw it with new eyes.

The old house had weathered a terrible hurricane yet it was still standing tall – just like Grandma and herself.

Deep down she knew that this 'fine Southern lady' would be their home again.

Acknowledgments

I owe a debt of gratitude to a great number of people; wonderful New Orleanians whose heroism in the face of the worst natural disaster ever to have been experienced in the United States, Hurricane Katrina, inspired me to write a book; Sr. Helen Prejean, my friend, author of "Dead Man Walking," who introduced me to her friend, Don Mullan, my publisher and friend who introduced me to his friend, Marita Conlon-McKenna, the renowned children's writer, author of the award-winning, "Under the Hawthorn Tree;" Marita helped me to stay focused on a story that I believed needed to be told; Jennifer Armstrong, my editor, whose comments were insightful and most helpful; Seamus Cashman for his valued professional advice; Clare Harkin whose sympathetic encouragement helped me to put on paper the pain in my heart; Joan O' Donovan and Maria Maguire who gave their untiring support as the journey began; Moya Nulty and the Sixth Class in St. Brigid's Primary School, Haddington Road, Dublin, convinced me that this American catastrophe had Irish appeal; James, Clodagh, Lisa, Lorna and Hannah helped me to get to know Jade better; Jean and Sherman Pittman offered me their home away from home in Baton Rouge, Louisiana, where Lynn Breaux, a proud New Orleanian, helped me with the local dialect; the many Dominicans who listened, read and empathized, especially the late Helen O' Dwyer whose enthusiasm for each chapter I wrote spurred me on to write the next one and whose belief, in my ability to write the book, never wavered; my brother, Brian, his wife, Ann and my sister, Angela, for their loving support through thick and thin and finally, my sister, Eileen, to whom I am indebted in ways far deeper than words can express.

Hurricane Katrina – the numbers

(as of October 20, 2005)

- Official death toll: 1,277
- Federal Aid: $62.3 billion
- People in New Orleans without privately owned transportation: 120,000
- American Red Cross shelters across 27 states: 1,150
- American Red Cross workers who provided relief aid: 190,000
- Fish that died at the New Orleans Aquarium of the Americas: 10,000
- Total number of evacuees: over 1 million.
- Lives saved by Coast Guard: 33,000
- Children separated from families by Hurricanes Katrina and Rita: 4,724
- MREs, ice and water brought in as of Oct. 20: 125 tons.
- Liters of water delivered to New Orleans as of Sept. 3: 7 million
- People inside Houston Astrodome by Sept. 3: 16,000
- E-mails CNN received from people searching for their relatives as of Sept.3: 15,000

(CNN REPORTS: KATRINA – STATE OF EMERGENCY, 2005)